MR. TOUCHDOWN

Mr. Touchdown

Lyda Phillips

iUniverse, Inc.
New York Bloomington

Mr. Touchdown

iUniverse books may be ordered through booksellers or by contacting:

iUniverse
1663 Liberty Drive
Bloomington, IN 47403
www.iuniverse.com
1-800-Authors (1-800-288-4677)

This is a work of fiction. All of the characters, names, incidents, organizations, and dialogue in this novel are either the products of the author's imagination or are used fictitiously.

ISBN: 978-1-60528-029-5 (pbk)
ISBN: 978-1-4401-0976-8 (cloth)
ISBN: 978-0-595-63271-8 (ebk)

Printed in the United States of America

This book is dedicated to Leola Thomas

ACKNOWLEDGMENTS

I would like to thank those who shared with me their stories of segregation, including my brother, Wim Phillips, and my friends Emily Pearce and Sue Allison. I'd like to acknowledge my debt to David Halberstam's *The Children*. And finally I'd like to pay tribute to all the children who by twos and threes and fours integrated Southern white schools in the 1950s and 1960s.

CHAPTER 1

▼

NOT HEROES

An old gray Ford hummed down Highway 61 heading south out of Memphis, Tennessee. The Mississippi River rolled by a few miles to the west. If the two Negro men in their dark suits and hats had kept driving a few miles farther south, they would have dropped down from the bluffs around Memphis onto the Mississippi Delta that stretched dead flat for hundreds of miles, a rich land of cotton and soybeans. Well, rich in some ways. The soil was rich, a few white folks were rich, but most people in the Delta were poor.

But the two men turned left off of Highway 61 onto Chickalissa Road, a two-lane paved road that cut between wide fields. Far off in the shimmering June heat they caught glimpses of bent figures chopping cotton. A mile or so down the road, the Ford turned right at a small red brick church onto a narrow dirt street.

In the middle of that street, Eddie Russell and his best friend, Vernell Cunningham, were throwing a football back and forth. School had been out just long enough for them to start to get bored. They watched the unfamiliar car ease off the paved road, raising a cloud of yellow dust. The dirt street was barely wide enough for the car. The two men inside stretched their necks looking for house numbers that weren't there. The neighborhood was better than a lot of Negro neighborhoods; most of the houses were painted, but they didn't have numbers. Everybody knew where everybody else lived.

Eddie watched the car coming toward them, then raised his eyebrow at Vernell, who shook his head. He didn't know them either. The car's bullet nose inched closer to where they stood, between Vernell's house and Eddie's Aunt Hattie's house.

Eddie threw the football hard into Vernell's chest. Vernell caught it and fired it onto his porch, making his sister and her friends in the porch swing shriek.

The car stopped, nearly touching Eddie's knees. He moved around to the driver's side, while Vernell eased over to the passenger's window.

"Where you goin'?" Eddie asked, overly polite.

"We are looking for the residence of Reverend Henry Russell," the driver answered, looking hard at Eddie like he knew Eddie was being a smart-ass. The man sounded like a stuck-up Northern Negro.

Eddie stepped back and waved a hand, allowing them to pass. "Three doors down on the right. Green house past the white house."

The car rolled forward and stopped three doors down. From the porch of Aunt Hattie's house, Eddie's sister, Lakeesha, commonly known as "Mouse," got up. She'd been curled up in a wicker chair reading, as usual. Mouse never hung out with the other girls. She was wrapped up in books, zipping away down her hole whenever anyone got too close. She annoyed Eddie. He wished she would act more like everybody else, hang out, laugh with the other girls. Mouse was just different, but she was his sister, so he had to defend her.

Lakeesha leaned over the porch rail and looked anxiously down the street at the Ford. Aunt Hattie, heavy in her porch rocker, grunted and got to her feet, too.

The men got out, walked to the door and knocked. The Reverend Henry Russell opened the door, shook both men's hands, and beckoned the visitors inside with a tight gesture. For a flicker of a second, Vernell went into his imitation of Reverend Russell's stiff, robot-like movements. Eddie bit back his laughter, not willing to laugh at his own father.

"Who *is* that?" Eddie called up to his aunt. She was only a few feet away. None of the houses had any front yards to speak of, just a bit of beaten grass and dirt.

Aunt Hattie made a disgusted snorting sound. "I don't know why Henry thinks he's got to do this," she said and went inside, slamming the screen door behind her.

Eddie and Vernell looked at each other, puzzled. Vernell's sister, Etta Lee, threw the football back to Eddie, an awkward dead-duck throw that started somewhere down around her knees. Eddie caught it and flipped the football, spinning, into the air.

Eddie threw to Vernell, watching the cluster of girls on Vernell's porch out of the corner of his eye, heard their light, high laughter. Vernell caught the ball, staggered back a few steps, exaggerating his stumbling, gratified by the girls' giggles.

"Goofball," Eddie said. Then they fell into a comfortable rhythm, a dance they'd danced for years. The girls went inside and for a while, the familiar *thunk, thunk* of the boys passing the football back and forth was the only human sound in the hot afternoon. A mockingbird sang loudly from the tangled hedges at the edge of the cotton field.

The front door of Eddie's house opened, and Reverend Russell's crisp voice called, "Son, come inside for a moment."

Eddie fired the ball one last time into Vernell's outstretched arms. Vernell twirled and ran, darting this way and that down the street, evading imaginary pursuit.

Eddie walked down to his house and followed his father into the living room. The men had removed their hats. The shorter, darker-skinned man's round glasses caught the light as he looked toward the door.

Eddie heard the back door open, then close, and figured Mouse had gone into her room the back way, down her safe hole.

After the bright June sun outside, the living room was dark, the air still and heavy on Eddie's skin. Empty coffee cups sat on the table among the crumbs of Mama's lemon cake. The tall man shut the brown leather briefcase and snapped it closed.

Eddie saw the two men recognize him from the encounter outside and exchange quick glances.

"Mel Collier from the NAACP," his father said, waving a hand at the tall man.

NAACP? Eddie thought. *What are they doing here?*

"Shelby Reed, from the Student Non-Violent Coordinating Committee," Reverend Russell continued, indicating the shorter, darker man. "My son, Eddie Russell."

Eddie shook hands formally with the two men.

"Eddie." His father looked down at the floor, his hands clasped as if he was praying. Eddie heard his mother moving around in the kitchen behind the living room.

"Eddie," Reverend Russell started again. "I'm going to ask you to do something very difficult. We want you to transfer to Forrest High School this fall."

Eddie saw sparks, like he'd been hit hard on the football field and lost consciousness for a few seconds. He sat down on the couch.

The two men studied Eddie as carefully as a couple of coaches, looking for signs of weakness. Reverend Russell lifted his glasses to wipe his face with his handkerchief. Eddie looked at his father in disbelief, but Reverend Russell looked away.

"What are you talking about?" Eddie asked the two strangers.

Mr. Collier held up a long sheet of paper, covered with typing. "This," he said, looking Eddie in the eye, daring him to say something smart, "is a desegregation order."

"You've been handpicked, Eddie," Mr. Reed said. "You're a good student, and you've demonstrated good self-control."

"And you're an athlete," Mr. Collier said. "That's very important."

"What's that got to do with it?"

"It gives you a place, a wedge to achieve acceptance in an all-white school," said his father.

Eddie opened his mouth, but Mr. Reed cut him off.

"We're not sure you can do this, Eddie. Your father has assured us you can, but if you go to that school, you must be like Gandhi. Do you know who Gandhi was?"

Eddie shrugged, half nodding. He knew who Gandhi was, but Mr. Reed rolled right on, not really looking at him.

"Gandhi changed the world by refusing to accept injustice, but he did it because he was absolutely committed to nonviolence." Mr. Reed's dark eyes bored into Eddie's.

Yeah, right, Eddie thought. *That might have worked in India or wherever, but here you'd get your head kicked in.*

"That's harder than it sounds," Mr. Reed said. The muscles of his jaw rippled. "It takes a great deal of courage to take blows from white men and not fight back. More courage than it takes to hit them back."

"Eddie, you are a football player, a basketball player," Mr. Collier said. "Those are violent, competitive sports. To be a star athlete you have to have a world of fight in you. Can you control that off the field?"

Eddie didn't answer.

"Can you do that, Eddie?" his father asked.

About two years ago, in 1963, Reverend Russell had taken a busload of church members to the March on Washington. Eddie had gone with him. Before they went, all of them had been taught how to endure taunts and jeers without reacting, how and when to sit down when the police told them to move, how to curl up and cover their heads with their hands if they were beaten.

But nothing like that had happened. They had been jammed in among thousands and thousands of other black folks far back in the crowd that day. The feeling of being pressed into that multitude of people had stayed with Eddie. He'd felt the anger in the crowd. Other people from the church had talked later about feeling hope rising up in them that day, but Eddie had only felt like somebody was choking him.

"Why didn't you tell me?" Eddie asked.

His father's eyes gleamed behind the glasses. He ignored Eddie's question, as Eddie had avoided his.

"Son, now is the time to find the strength to endure, to triumph. Nothing is more powerful than a righteous idea," he said.

Eddie looked down at his ragged Converse high-tops. Then he got up to face the men. He refused to sit like a child in a corner being lectured by adults.

You're not asking me to do this, are you? You're telling me, he thought, looking at his father's still face. For a horrible second he thought he might cry over the unfairness of it. His junior year, star running back, all his friends, everything familiar, gone in an instant. He would be nothing at Forrest. Less than nothing—despised, hated. All because of Dr. King's damned dream.

The men watched him apprehensively. He tried to say, "No." He tried to object, to argue, to plead, but one look into his father's eyes, and he knew it was useless. The train had already left the station.

"What's going to happen?" he asked.

Mr. Reed and Mr. Collier looked at each other. Eddie caught a flicker of relief in their eyes.

"You can't expect even one act of kindness," said Mr. Reed, "not one. If you don't expect any kindness, it won't bother you so much when you don't get it."

"You must keep your head down, don't make trouble, don't bump into people, keep your distance and don't expect to make friends," Mr. Collier said.

"And you must never so much as look a white girl in the face," Mr. Reed said. "That will get you hurt faster than anything you can do. They don't exist. Remember that. They are invisible to you, as you will be invisible to them."

They sounded like they had made this speech before. Eddie started to tune them out.

His father held up his hand, stopping the two younger men in their tracks.

"You must look into the soul of your enemies and find in them something to love," Reverend Russell said, his eyes cold.

Eddie looked from one man to another. How could his father have broken it to him like this, in front of strangers, giving him no choice, no say in it at all? He might actually have chosen to go fight for Dr. King's dream if he'd been brought into the decision, but his father hadn't trusted him. He'd set him up, trapped him.

"Can I play football?" he asked.

*   *   *   *

Eddie sat on the couch. His heart pounded, and his thighs quivered. He wished he could get away. His mother had come in and now sat beside him, patting his arm. Eddie looked in her face and saw that she too had submitted to the inevitability of his father's decision. But the quick flash of understanding in her eyes comforted him.

"Esther, we'd better get Lakeesha."

With a sigh that caught in her throat, his mother got up and went into the kitchen.

"Lakeesha?" Eddie asked in amazement. "You're not going to—"

His father held up a hand to stop him from speaking. Eddie looked at the floor, seething. The door to the porch opened, and he heard a rattle as his mother pulled aside the curtain that separated Lakeesha's bedroom from the rest of the porch.

"Keesha, baby? Your father wants to see you," Eddie heard her say.

Lakeesha stumbled into the living room, looking lost and sleepy, the way she always did when they pulled her out of her books. When she saw the two strange men and Eddie, she stopped, stood up straight, the fog vanishing from her eyes. Her whole body tensed. Eddie's fists clenched. There was no hole for Lakeesha to disappear into.

"Lakeesha, daughter," Reverend Russell began and then stopped speaking.

Mr. Collier looked at him and quickly started speaking. "Lakeesha, this is Shelby Reed from SNCC." He pronounced it the way they all did, *snick,* like a lock closing. "And I am Mel Collier from the NAACP. We have obtained a court order to desegregate Forrest High School this fall. You and Eddie, and two other girls, Lethe Jefferson and Rochelle Perry, have been chosen to desegregate the school."

Lakeesha's eyes darted from one man to another.

Say, no. Say, NO! Eddie thought at her.

"What's 'snick'?" she asked in a small voice.

Eddie wanted to scream with frustration. Lakeesha hadn't even for one second thought about saying, "No," to their father. At least he had considered it—for a second.

"The Student Non-Violent Coordinating Committee," Mr. Reed said. Eddie hated his condescending smile, like he felt sorry for anyone who didn't know what SNCC was. Lakeesha leaned back from the two men. She shot a quick glance at Eddie, then stared down at her feet.

"What will they do to us?" she asked.

Eddie swallowed and closed his eyes, images from television flickering across his memory. Screaming whites, their faces twisted, as frightened children walked down the sidewalk to school guarded by white men holding guns.

The adults were all silent, too. Everyone in the room held their breath.

Then Mr. Collier stepped toward Lakeesha, bending down to get to her eye level. He took her hand.

"Lakeesha, this is not Little Rock. We've had ten long years of foot-dragging since then, but I truly believe there will be no trouble like that."

"Selma broke the back of white resistance." Mr. Reed's voice grated on Eddie's ears. He talked too loud, too clipped, like he was reading a proclamation. "We'll have a Voting Rights Act before the end of the summer. We're winning."

Mr. Collier looked at Mr. Reed with a frown. Eddie thought he was trying to tone Mr. Reed down, warn him to go slow.

"We will work with all of you for the rest of the summer on this—what to expect, how to behave," Mr. Collier said, his voice soft and gentle, but Eddie didn't trust him either. "You four and the Negro students who will be desegregating other white schools this fall—you will be ready."

Mr. Reed handed Lakeesha a page from a newspaper.

"This is Diane Nelson. I was with her at Fisk University when we started the lunch counter sit-ins in Nashville. She's gone to jail over and over again. Diane Nelson is a hero, Lakeesha. You will be a hero too."

The faded newspaper clipping shook in Lakeesha's hand.

So! This Mr. Reed had been in the sit-in movement, Eddie thought. That had led to the Freedom Rides, to riots, to people being beaten and killed, to little girls about Lakeesha's age being blown up at church, and finally to him and his little sister being "chosen" to desegregate Forrest High.

Eddie got up and crossed the room to his sister, looked down at the picture in her hand. Diane Nelson, this hero, a beautiful light-skinned, light-eyed Negro woman, stared defiantly at the camera, holding a baby in her arms.

Eddie put his arm around Lakeesha's shoulders, felt her whole body shivering. His mother's eyes were closed. She was praying, he knew.

Eddie turned and glared at the older men, at his father.

"You all want us to go to an all-white school, we'll go," he said. "But don't expect us to be heroes."

CHAPTER 2

▼

TWO, FOUR, SIX, EIGHT, WE DON'T WANT TO INTEGRATE

A mile or so from Eddie's house, in a leafy neighborhood of wide green lawns and big white houses, Nancy Martin lay face down on her bed, propped up on her elbows, a battered copy of Kenneth Patchen's epic poem *The Journal of Albion Moonlight* open in front of her. The spine of the book was patched with masking tape. Her red-gold hair hung over her eyes and her lips moved soundlessly as she read.

> *I know more than Apollo*
> *For oft when he lies sleeping*
> *I see the stars at mortal wars*
> *In the wounded welkin weeping.*

The front door slammed downstairs.

"Nancy!" Sally Hughes called, her footsteps pounding on the polished wood of the stairs. She lived just three doors down and had been in and out of Nancy's house like family since they were old enough to walk.

Their neighborhood was old, the houses rambled and had odd corners and unexpected windows. They had played in the fields behind the houses all their lives. Sally even had horses that they rode bareback over the fields and along the quiet paved streets.

Nancy's house was the last one on the street. A quarter of a mile down it crossed a railroad track and then turned to dirt, wound around some bare hillocks and dry fields and then ended up at the back end of the Negro neighborhood where their maid Hattie lived.

Nancy's father sometimes complained about the trains, but Nancy secretly loved the sound of the fast City of New Orleans passenger train as it passed by every night at about 10 o'clock and wailed like Hank Williams' song, "I'm so lonesome I could cry."

Nancy and Sally had gone through everything together, kindergarten, Sunday School, they'd been cheerleaders together since the seventh grade. Now they were going to be juniors when school opened again in three more days. But in the last few months, Nancy had found there were some things she didn't want Sally to know about.

Nancy reached down and shoved *The Journal of Albion Moonlight* under her bed just as Sally burst into the room, her face red from running in the heat.

"You'll never *believe* what's happening!"

Nancy sat up and wrapped her arms around her legs.

"What?"

"They're going to integrate Forrest this fall! A boy and three girls, juniors and sophomores."

Nancy felt a shock through her whole body. She sat up straighter on her bed. "No! That's incredible!"

Sally flopped down on a blue-and-white striped chair in the corner of Nancy's room and then shot up again, rubbing her bare, freckled leg.

"Ooh, fudge!" Sally picked up the album cover she had sat on and wrinkled her nose. "How can you listen to that Bob Dylan? He sounds like somebody stepped on a cat."

Without stopping for breath, she went on, "I don't know why on earth those colored people are doing this. It just doesn't make any sense at all. Why are they pushing themselves in where they're not wanted? It's terrible."

Nancy was silent. On television, she had seen blacks being beaten and blasted with water from fire hoses in Alabama. Little girls had been blown up in a church. She'd seen dogs attacking black marchers. Her father had been outraged, and her mother had called him a Yankee and told him he didn't understand how things were down here.

Nancy had sided with her father in this argument, as she usually did when her parents sparred. The things ugly white people were doing outraged her, too. But she kept her feelings to herself around her friends and pretended to feel like they did. For a minute she tried to imagine going to school with Negroes and then laughed.

Sally looked annoyed. "What are you laughing at?"

"I just imagined going to school with a bunch of colored people but they were all grown-up, like sitting in a class with Agnes and Hattie."

"It's not funny, Nancy. These won't be our maids; they'll be kids our age. God knows what they'll be like."

"I guess they might be poor," Nancy said.

"And dirty," Sally said.

"They're always saying they just want their rights but I can't see what going to school with us has to do with that," Nancy said.

"They don't want their rights," Sally said indignantly. "They want our rights."

"What's going to happen?" Nancy asked. "I don't want all those National Guard troops and dogs watching us go to school."

"I don't think there's a thing we can do about it, so I, for one, am going to pretend like it's not happening at all," Sally said with a regal lift of her chin.

"That might be hard," Nancy said.

"Our last two years of high school are going to be ruined. It'll just be completely distracting."

They sat in silence for a few minutes. Nancy looked at Sally's unhappy face, the platinum blond hair with a faint streak of green in it from the chlorine at the pool, trying to think of a way to make Sally laugh, make her feel better. It seemed like she'd been comforting Sally her whole life.

When they were about three years old, Sally had gotten stung by a bee at Sunday School. She had screamed and cried, her face turning a brilliant red. Nancy had been terrified and cried too, but everyone said she'd been hugging Sally and trying to make her stop wailing. Nancy only remembered Sally's red face and open mouth, her first memory. They'd been friends ever since, climbing trees, building forts in the fields behind Nancy's house, playing mystery in the attic of Sally's house, playing Spin the Bottle at their first boy-girl parties. She laughed again.

"What?" Sally asked, annoyed.

"I was just thinking about that time you got stung by the bee."

"Oh, stop! Nobody will ever let me forget that." But Sally was smiling again, and finally laughed too.

"So, should we go to the club, you think?"

"Sure, let me go ask Mom," Nancy said.

On the way to the club in Sally's new baby-blue Mustang, Sally and Nancy passed unpainted houses where black children played in bare dirt front yards, chickens and dogs dodging in and out among them.

"Look!" said Sally. "Can you imagine going to school with them?"

"No, I can't."

They pulled through the stone gates of the Club, zipping past the last two holes of the golf course. As they ran up the walk past the rambling clubhouse to the swimming pool, the smell of chlorine stung Nancy's nose and the sun beat down on her bare shoulders.

In the pool, Maryanne Wilson executed a perfect dive. Maryanne, who was 4-foot-9, wore a size four shoe and a size two dress, made Nancy feel like a clod. She sat down with a sigh at a table under the umbrella. She and Sally put their bright-colored swimming pool bags down on a chair and pulled out their bottles of baby oil with iodine mixed in to give their pale skin more color. Neither of them could get a decent tan.

Sally jabbed Nancy with a pink fingernail. Spencer Smith, a towel around his neck, his big feet in ancient penny loafers, his vast swimming trunks billowing, stood next to the snack bar.

"There's the blimp," Sally said in a loud whisper.

Spencer saw the jab and heard the whisper. Nancy smiled at him to take away the sting. He flicked his towel in her direction and winked.

Clifford, a gangly black teenager, his hair processed in thick waves, pushed a hamburger on a paper plate through the window of the club's snack bar to Spencer and turned up the radio.

Clifford lived down the street and around the corner from Eddie and Lakeesha. He was going with Rochelle Perry, who was also going to be integrating Forrest in a few weeks and he really didn't like that idea, though he knew quite well that if anyone could handle the experience, it was Rochelle.

He was a senior at Douglass High School, played tight end. Clifford was good enough, big enough to play college ball. With his height and his long arms he made the kind of target a quarterback loved. Of course, none of these Southern high schools, white or black, had much of a passing game. They played traditional, no-risk offenses, a line of big kids in front, with the quarterback behind center and two running backs behind him on either side.

Clifford could have dreamed of going on to play football in college, even professionally, but he didn't. He didn't have the grades, the money or the desire to go to college. Instead he was flipping burgers for the white kids at the country club and glad to have the job.

"*Mashed potato, yeah, yeah,*" Clifford sang to himself.

"Come on, Clifford, show us the Mashed Potato!" Spencer said, putting his hamburger down on the table next to Sally and Nancy.

Spencer flung down his towel and held out his hand to Nancy. She and Sally both got up and they all three danced around the table. Clifford came out of the kitchen, laughing.

"It's like putting out a cigarette on the floor." His feet flew across the concrete.

"I can't *do* it," wailed Sally, her hair falling into her face.

"Like this." Spencer's feet slipped from side to side, arms out to his sides like wings to keep his balance.

"Naw, your feet are doing the Mashed Potato, but your arms are flapping like a bird," laughed Clifford. "Like this." Again Clifford slid across the concrete. Spencer, in slick-soled loafers, followed him, graceful despite his bulk. He grabbed Nancy's hand, and she fluttered across the concrete with him, her bare feet burning from the friction.

They grinned at each other, remembering their many triumphs on the dance floor, ever since they had first starting going to parties together in the fifth grade. They both loved to dance.

The song ended, Spencer slapped Clifford on the back, and he went back into his shack, which he called his office, and turned the radio down a notch.

"I've got to go in. I'm dying." Sally dashed for the pool, cutting into the water in a shallow dive. Nancy followed, swimming under the rope that marked the deep end before she pulled herself up onto the side next to Sally.

Spencer lumbered down the diving board, jumped, hit the groaning board once for takeoff. He flew into the air and came down in a cannonball that splashed water onto the girls.

"Oooh," Sally screeched, shaking the water out of her eyes.

"Spencer Smith, why aren't you at football practice? School starts in a week, and ya'll should be practicing." She flipped water at him with her foot.

Spencer stood on the bottom of the six-foot section, his chin easily clearing the water, drops of water beading on his burned, peeling nose. Maryanne dived again, perfect as usual, and climbed out of the pool to sit next to Sally.

"Coach canceled practice today because of Eddie Russell, you know, the colored guy."

Spencer suddenly had their full attention.

"You know, the colored boy who's going to school with us. He's a football player. Coach is working with him today."

"Oh, my, God!" said Sally.

"Flip me, Spencer," Maryanne ordered, hopping off the side of the pool onto Spencer's broad, tanned shoulders. He gave the tiny girl a flip. She dove headfirst into the water.

"I'm going to St. Anne's next year," Maryanne said when she surfaced. "Daddy doesn't want me going to school with Negroes." She drawled out the first "e" in Negroes in a mocking, insulting whine. Nancy wanted to push her head back under the water.

"Think he's there now, the colored boy, at the football field?" Sally asked.

Spencer shrugged.

Sally looked at Nancy.

"I think we need to check this out," she said.

The girls gathered their things. Nancy grabbed her striped bag, hopping from one bare foot to the other on the sizzling concrete.

"Hey, there's Larry," Sally whispered.

Nancy looked up and saw her ex-boyfriend Larry "Touchdown" Townsend sauntering up the walk toward the pool. He was tall, blond, blue eyes, wide shoulders, narrow hips, star quarterback. Nancy couldn't believe she used to think he was a god.

"Oh, sugar!" Nancy straightened up with a jerk. Larry's blue eyes met hers in a hard stare. She looked away.

"Come on! Let's go!" Nancy said urgently to Sally.

"Go where?" Larry drawled, still staring at Nancy.

"Larry!" They heard Maryanne's high voice. She pranced up and locked her arm through Larry's. "Come on. Everyone's leaving. I need somebody to play with." She pulled him away.

"Hey," yelled Spencer. "Give me a ride home."

"All right. Hurry up," Sally said.

"Shotgun," yelled Nancy as they ran across the parking lot.

Spencer wedged himself into the back seat.

"Got enough room back there?" Sally taunted him. Nancy glanced back and saw Larry staring after the car. She shuddered, like when her mother said a possum was walking over your grave.

And then the Mustang tore off toward the high school, top down, "I Want to Hold Your Hand," blaring on the radio. They all sang at the top of their lungs.

Nathan Bedford Forrest High School had five big buildings, two of them full of machine shops. It had an agricultural program with a greenhouse and rows of experimental crops. A few World War II vintage airplanes were parked behind the stadium for the shop boys to take apart and put back together.

Sally slowed on the narrow road behind the stadium near the airplanes. A black kid, in a soaked gray T-shirt and black shorts, ran in the blazing sun at the far end of the cinder track. A black man stood next to Coach Roy Ezell, dwarfing him in width if not in height.

Sally pulled slowly off to the side of the road, turned off the radio and they all watched, fascinated. The boy finished a lap and stopped in front of the two men. Coach Ezell made some gestures.

"Who's that colored man?" asked Sally. "Are we going to have Negro teachers, too?"

Spencer squinted at the black man. "Naw, that's the Douglass coach, I think. Jim Frazier. He was a big star at Grambling. Boy, he must be mad about losing Eddie Russell."

"How do you know so much?" Sally asked.

"I read the paper, Sal. You all jump around a lot at football games. Should read the sports section sometime, find out what's going on."

"Oh, you!" Sally snapped back at him. "I know why you know so much. Your daddy works with Negroes."

"Yep, that he does."

"Sally!" said Nancy. "Spencer's daddy is a foreman. He doesn't work *with* Negroes. They work *for* him."

"What's the difference?" Spencer said easily.

Nancy examined Spencer for a moment, then looked back out at the football field.

The colored boy began throwing his body at the blocking bags. They could hear his sharp grunts and the sound of his shoulder hitting the sandbag.

"That's his name? Eddie Russell?" Nancy asked.

Spencer nodded.

"And we're going to have to cheer for that?" Sally hissed.

"I guess so," said Nancy, leaning her cheek on her hand and her elbow on the dashboard, staring at Eddie. She thought of Clifford. Had he heard Maryanne talking that way about Neeee-groes?

*   *   *   *

Out on the field, sweat ran down Eddie's back, and his heart pounded. He leaned over, hands on his knees, pulling in painful gulps of thick, humid air. When he straightened up, the white man's face wavered. Coach Frazier's voice rumbled behind him, but Eddie couldn't understand the words over the roaring in his head.

His eyes finally focused and locked with Coach Ezell's pale blue eyes. Coach Ezell ran a thick hand over his black crew cut and twisted his mouth in a satisfied smirk.

"Not in too good shape, are you, boy?"

Eddie's head swam again, this time with rage. Run five miles on a boiling cinder track in 95-degree heat and then half an hour banging into the bags? Not in good shape? This redneck had never seen shape like his.

"Oh, and by the way, Russell, I already ordered all the football jackets last spring. You ain't going to have one."

Eddie looked up, his eyes dark and red.

Coach Frazier's heavy hand fell on his shoulder. "Let's go, Eddie. I'll run you home."

Eddie turned without a word and walked over to the benches that lined the practice field. He grabbed his bag, heaved it over his shoulder and walked toward Coach Frazier's car, his breath burning his lungs.

Coach Frazier started the car in silence. Eddie put his arm out of the window and then jerked it off the hot metal. He leaned his head back and sighed.

"Rough," Coach Frazier said, backing the car down the cinder track. He shifted to drive, and they shot away, raising a trail of dust that Eddie hoped was choking Coach Ezell.

"Right," Eddie said.

They looked at each other, and then Eddie looked out the window at the fields and houses whipping by, and his coach looked back at the road.

"He called me 'boy,'" Eddie said.

"They gone call you lots worse than that before this is over."

Eddie's silence filled the car.

"Eddie, you been a king at Douglass. You been a prince all your life. Now think of it like you're going into exile. Like you're going on a quest on behalf of your people."

"Right."

"Seriously, son, you can't go back now. You got to make that redneck eat his words. This is big-time high school football. Forrest won the state championship two years ago. This could be a big opportunity for you."

"If I play."

Coach Frazier glanced over at Eddie.

"Right, if you play."

CHAPTER 3

▼

NOT EQUAL

As his father's car drove slowly up to the high school, Eddie saw the cheerleaders practicing on the front lawn of the big yellow brick building. A bushy-haired, freckled girl jumped at the point of a V of cheerleaders facing the highway. Cars honked, people waved. The cheerleaders kept working, sweating, in blue shorts and gold sleeveless T-shirts.

Eddie thought the cheers strange, with sharp, stiff arm movements and barked out words. He was used to cheerleaders who danced on the sidelines, loose and graceful.

> *We're the champs,*
> *(clap, clap)*
> *We're the champs,*
> *(clap, clap)*
> *We're the C-H-A-M-P-S, Yes!*
> *(clap)*
> *We're the best,*
> *(clap, clap)*

The car doors opened, and the cheerleaders stopped to stare at them. Mr. Jefferson's car pulled in behind them, and Lethe and Rochelle got out. They made quite a crowd—four black students with their parents, ten people of various shades of brown.

The four of them had been working together off and on all summer. Eddie thought Lethe and Rochelle would do all right. Rochelle could sass back at anybody and Lethe was the smartest person Eddie had ever met. He looked at Lakeesha, who was tight against her mother's side. Mouse was definitely their weak link. He felt the same surge of anger he had felt ever since the day his father had made The Announcement, as they all now called it. As usual he didn't know whether he was mad at Lakeesha for being so pathetic or his father for putting her through this.

A white man stood on the steps of the school next to one of the two stone urns that flanked the front door. His legs were apart, his arms crossed, nose red, hazel eyes hard and cold. Eddie remembered a picture of a white man with a baseball bat blocking the doors of a school. All this man lacked was the bat.

His father walked calmly up to the white man. As they all got closer, the white man seemed to shrink. He wasn't so big, not nearly as tall as Rochelle's father, who was a huge man, somewhat stooped, dressed in work clothes, unlike Reverend Russell or Lethe Perry's father, who wore suits. One of his big, callused hands rested on his tall daughter's shoulder. Rochelle leaned very slightly against him.

Reverend Russell did not offer to shake hands with the white man, who they had been told was Mr. Stanton, the Forrest principal.

"Mr. Stanton, I am Reverend Henry Russell. This is my son, Eddie, and my daughter, Lakeesha, my wife, Mrs. Russell."

Eddie looked sideways at the cheerleaders watching with their mouths open. He smiled to himself. He'd be giving them a lot to stare at this year.

"And this is Lethe Jefferson, her father Mr. Jefferson, Mrs. Jefferson." Eddie's father continued his polite introductions. "Rochelle Perry, Mr. Perry, Mrs. Perry."

Mr. Stanton nodded at each person Reverend Russell introduced, a short, sharp nod. As he finished the introductions, a small blond woman hurried out of the school. She rushed up to Reverend Russell and shook his hand furiously.

"I'm Gloria Granger, the guidance counselor. It's so wonderful to meet you, Mr. Russell."

Lethe, a round girl with round glasses, blinked at the energetic white woman and looked sideways at Eddie. As Mrs. Granger turned, Rochelle backed up a half step, her thin face tight with distrust.

"Are you Lakeesha?" Mrs. Granger asked.

"No, I'm Rochelle."

"Rochelle! So happy to meet you, dear. Now which one of you is Lakeesha?"

Lakeesha, standing close to her mother, reluctantly half-raised her hand. "Ah, Lakeesha. And that must mean you are Lethe, dear."

Mrs. Granger pronounced the name wrong, making it rhyme with "death," when it was actually two syllables, Lee-the. Lethe nodded, her head to one side, and didn't try to correct the mistake. Mrs. Granger's blue eyes slid across Lethe and lit briefly on Eddie.

"And of course you are Eddie, our football player!" Mrs. Granger chirped.

"Yes, ma'am," said Eddie. He took a half-step forward to shake her hand, but Mrs. Granger jumped backward.

"Come inside everyone, and let's get this paperwork done. Classes to pick, need to get that out of the way!"

As they trooped into the building behind the chattering Mrs. Granger, Lakeesha grabbed Eddie's arm and pulled him back behind the others.

"That girl, that cheerleader over there, the one with the reddish hair, she's Nancy Martin."

Eddie didn't get it.

"Aunt Hattie works for the Martins."

Eddie raised his eyebrows. Yes, that was true. He hadn't been aware that the Martins had a daughter who was a cheerleader. He still didn't get why Lakeesha seemed so unhinged about it though.

"Eddie! She's given us all *clothes*!"

Oh, a clothes thing. For years Hattie and the other women who worked for white families had been bringing home sacks of clothes that they distributed throughout the neighborhood. Eddie struggled to understand Lakeesha's new panic and then got a flicker of it. How would it feel to wear that cheerleader's clothes when she might see you in them?

"That's okay, Mouse. You'll just have to let Etta Lee wear them, I guess."

Lakeesha gave him one of those girl looks, the ones that shout, "you don't get anything, do you?" although it was diluted by her nervousness. They hurried after the others.

The musty smell of the school swept over Eddie as they went through the doors into the dim hallway. It smelled nothing like Frederick Douglass, where he had gone since the first grade. Douglass had a softer smell, more fresh air. The grass outside Douglass was longer and softer. Trees grew right up to the windows, enclosing the school in leafy shadows. A blast of homesickness knotted his stomach.

They crowded into the narrow space before the high counter in the school office, where a window air conditioner loudly pumped a wisp of cool air into the room. Mrs. Granger, still talking, rustled papers and distributed forms for the students and their parents to fill out.

"There's not going to be any trouble," Mr. Stanton said abruptly. He glared at the clock on the wall behind them, not looking any of them in the eye. Then with a last stern look over the tops of his glasses at the door to the hall, Mr. Stanton retreated into his private office and solidly shut the door.

Mrs. Granger sighed as the door closed, and Mr. Perry shifted his big body back toward the wall. Eddie took the pile of papers Mrs. Granger handed him and looked down at Lakeesha. His sister's sweating hands left damp marks on the polished wood of the counter.

Faintly outside he could hear the cheerleaders chanting again.

> *We're the champs,*
> *(clap, clap)*
> *We're the champs,*
> *(clap, clap)*

"Now, Lethe and Lakeesha, let's see, you two girls are sophomores, aren't you? Eddie and Rochelle are our juniors!" She beamed proudly at them.

"Yes, ma'am," Eddie said. His eyes microscopically rolled up as he looked at Lakeesha. A smile flitted across her tense face and vanished.

"Well, if I might make some recommendations, I'd say we put Eddie down for some good solid vocational-technical courses—shop, maybe? And we'll get you sophomore girls in Algebra I, English, and Basic Science, for your required courses and maybe Home Economics, and one other class—how about World History or Spanish?" She smiled at Lethe, her pen poised over the form.

Lethe was silent, her lower lip moved forward just slightly. A heavy silence radiated from the adults.

"I believe that is the standard course of study for a freshman at Forrest," said Mr. Jefferson. "Am I correct?"

Mrs. Granger glanced up at Mr. Jefferson, looking at him directly for the first time. Eddie looked over, trying to see him through Mrs. Granger's eyes—the suit and tie, his tortoise shell glasses, the immaculate white shirt. Eddie stifled a snort of laughter at the confused look on her face.

"Maybe I could save you some time if I gave you these students' transcripts," Reverend Russell said calmly. "I had them sent in earlier this summer, but I know you must have been very busy."

He carefully unfolded a sheaf of papers from his pocket and slid it across the counter to Mrs. Granger. Eddie saw Lakeesha rise a bit onto her toes and strain for a glimpse at Lethe's transcript. She'd always been dying to see Lethe's report card. Eddie could see it easily from his height. As he expected, a blaze of A's filled all the boxes.

"We have thought long and hard about which of our children we would ask to come to this school," Reverend Russell continued. "We picked our best and brightest. They can do any work you give them. They will enroll in their grade-level classes, and they will do well. I can assure you of that."

Mrs. Granger looked doubtful.

"All right," she said. "I know you all will do your very best, of course, but if at any time you find the work to be just too much for you, that you're just the teeniest bit behind, come to me. We'll just quietly take care of it, put you into classes where you'd be more comfortable. You all have not been in a school as challenging as Forrest."

"Grade-level classes," said Mr. Jefferson.

"Mrs. Granger, is that your name?" asked Mrs. Perry.

Mrs. Granger nodded her curly blond head.

"My daughter works hard. All these children work hard. You give them the chance. They'll show you their quality."

Mrs. Granger still looked doubtful, with the super-friendly expression locked on her face. A heavy silence stretched out. Lakeesha shifted uneasily next to Eddie.

"I'd like to take shop," Eddie said.

They all stared at him, and then Reverend Russell laughed, without warmth. "All right, Eddie, take shop. It's good to know how to make things. But you'll take your college preparatory courses, too."

Mrs. Granger began to write, while they all watched. Eddie was a little disappointed. He would have liked to slide back into familiar English and math, take it easy, but no one in Reverend Russell's family was allowed to take things easy.

When the paperwork was finished at last, Mrs. Granger showed them around the school, taking them from the New Building, where the office was, to the Old Building with its worn wooden floors and pipes crisscrossing the ceiling. Eddie tried to imagine 1,200 students in this monstrous complex. Douglass High School had only 400 students.

She guided them to their classrooms, showed them where the bathrooms were, and took them through the echoing cafeteria and gymnasiums, one for the girls and a bigger one for the boys. The home economics rooms smelled like cakes and disinfectant. An array of microscopes lined the tables of the biology lab in a separate one-story science building. Colorful anatomy and periodical table charts hung on the walls. Lakeesha lingered in the doorway as the adults made their way back outside.

"They have so much stuff!" she whispered.

"Separate, but not equal," Rochelle said.

Eddie laughed. Rochelle grinned at him.

Finally as they left the school, Mrs. Granger took Lethe's hand. "Lethe, dear, you mustn't be disappointed if you don't do quite as well here at Forrest as you did at Douglass. I know you'll understand."

Eddie wondered if someone should tell her how to pronounce Lethe's name, but decided he didn't want to be the one to do it.

Mrs. Granger let go of Lethe's hand and turned to Lakeesha. "Lakeesha, if you ever have any problems at all, even if you just want to talk to somebody, come to me. I really want to help."

Eddie grabbed Rochelle's arm and pulled her with him down the stairs to avoid any awful good-bye speech from Mrs. Granger. He looked back to see her giving Lakeesha a pat on the shoulder.

"Phony bitch," Rochelle hissed in Eddie's ear.

"Yep, she is that all right."

Even though the air was so humid it felt like he was breathing underwater, Eddie was glad to be outside again. He sucked in the sweet smell of cut grass that the cheerleaders had trampled under their feet.

Lakeesha caught up with them and looked back at Mrs. Granger, who waggled her hand at them from the steps.

"It's okay, little sister," Eddie whispered, putting his hand on her shoulder and propelling her toward the car. "You'll make it." *Phony bitch or no phony bitch*, he thought.

He opened the door for her and his mother to get into the car. A wave of hot air rushed at him like a blast furnace. "Have a good practice, son," his Mama said as he closed the door.

"I'll try," Eddie said.

✳   ✳   ✳   ✳

By the time the black students and their families left, the cheerleaders had drifted down the lawn toward the gym. Nancy and Sally were talking to Spencer and Bobby Davidson, who were on their way to football practice.

"There they go," Bobby said.

The girls whirled around and watched the Negroes file out of the school and get into their cars. The colored boy closed the door to one of the cars and began walking toward them down the long sidewalk.

"That nigger's going to be a real pain in the ass," Bobby said.

Nancy invisibly winced at the word. Her mother had always told her ladies didn't use it. Her mother was a bore about all that, of course, but nevertheless, it sounded coarse. She was a little surprised at Bobby. She'd known him since the third grade but had never heard him talk about Negroes at all. Now he seemed really angry.

"Coach giving him a real hard time," Spencer said.

"Hoping he'll quit," said Bobby.

"He's not going to quit," Spencer said. "And actually he's pretty good."

"How good could he be, coming from that crummy school?" Bobby said. "Coach says he'll never be up to our level. You watch! Coach won't play him."

The boys walked away as Eddie got closer. Nancy and Sally hurried away, too, toward the Old Building. As they crossed the parking lot, a red Corvair pulled up beside them. Larry leaned out and handed

Nancy a red rose. He smiled at her, but she handed the rose back and walked on, quickly getting onto the sidewalk. The Corvair roared away with a screech.

"Oh, Nancy, that was so romantic about Larry!"

"Romantic! It's creepy!" Nancy shuddered. "I wish he'd leave me alone."

"Why? He still loves you, Nancy!"

"No, he doesn't. He just wants to—" She stopped and looked helplessly at Sally.

"What? Go all the way?" Sally shrugged. "They all do. That's no reason to break up."

"It wasn't that."

"Well, what then?"

"I can't talk about it, Sally. I really can't."

In silence they walked up the steps into the dim hall, slightly cooler than in the hot sun.

"So, who *do* you want to go out with this fall?"

"I've got my eye on Spencer Smith."

"Spencer! After you went out with Larry for two years? You're kidding, Nancy! He's a tackle. A cheerleader can't go out with a tackle."

"Actually he's a guard, not a tackle."

"That's kind of sort of a tackle. He's as big as a barn and about that bright."

"No, I think he's more about the size of an upright freezer."

"Maybe a grain silo."

"A truck, a Mack truck. Big is good. Very good."

They laughed.

"But Wayne Rogers wants to ask you out," Sally said.

"Bo-ring," she said.

"He's the president of the junior class, Nancy."

"Big deal. I already have other plans."

"Not adventurous enough for you, huh?"

"Right. Can't see him in Greenwich Village."

"Playing bongos!"

They screamed with laughter at the ridiculous image of serious Wayne Rogers playing the bongos in a smoky, beatnik jazz club, glasses slipping down his nose.

Sally pushed the bathroom door open, and they found Mrs. Granger at the sink. The hot water steamed, and soap bubbles foamed. When the girls left, after washing the sweat from their faces and re-doing their makeup, Mrs. Granger was still at the sink, washing her hands.

*   *   *   *

At practice, the football team played in pads for the first time, sweltering in the steaming afternoon sun. They did jumping jacks, push-ups, stretches, running in place, the stripes on the field newly painted and the grass thick and green under their cleats. Eddie fell into the familiar rhythm of practice, his mind altogether blank.

Until he heard Townsend's loud, rather high voice, asking, "Coach, can I move?"

Everyone stopped. Townsend, next to Eddie, looked at him, his nose wrinkled up behind the single bar on his helmet. The silence thickened until the only sound Eddie could hear was the blood pounding in his ears. He looked right into Townsend's eyes. Townsend looked away.

Coach Ezell nodded and jerked his chin to the right. With a grin at Eddie, Townsend trotted down to the other end of the line, whispering, "Nigger school," as he went past.

Eddie stood, isolated on the field.

"All right, back to work. One. Two," Coach Ezell barked, and they began jumping jacks again.

The team's pace, though, was ragged.

"All right, knock off," Coach yelled. "Into the locker room, you bunch of lead-assed losers. You, Russell, two laps!"

The other boys, groaning and panting, trotted off the field toward the gym and the locker rooms, yanking off their helmets. Eddie stood silent, his breath coming easily still.

Coach looked up, feigning surprise. "Russell, I think I said two laps."

Eddie took off his helmet.

"I don't think I gave you permission to take your helmet off, boy. Get moving."

Eddie yanked his helmet back on and moved out onto the cinder track, began to jog. After two laps, his anger still burning bright, he walked toward the gym. Already some of the white boys were getting into their parents' cars or walking away down the sidewalk. Slowly Eddie opened the locker room door.

Suddenly, he realized what this was all about. It was the first time they had changed clothes in the locker room. Spencer, still in his undershorts and T-shirt, scrubbed his tanned face with a damp towel, but most of the white boys scurried out, with nervous glances his way.

Without a word, Eddie went to his locker, which was in a row by itself at the very back. Slowly he stripped off his helmet, pads, uniform. He tried to empty his mind but found himself thinking about that day two weeks ago when Coach Ezell had first called him "boy."

Wrapping a towel around himself, Eddie walked to the empty showers. Spencer banged the door of his locker. Eddie, standing bare-footed on the damp, cool concrete floor heard the door close behind him. Water dripped slowly from one of the showerheads. Eddie took one deep shuddering breath, then stood up straighter, threw his towel over the bar, and turned on the water.

CHAPTER 4

▼

THE JACKET

On the first day of school, Eddie jumped out of his father's car with his gym bag in his hand. Lakeesha followed slowly.

There were no crowds of yelling white people. No dogs. No chanting. No spitting. The police were there, though, two troopers' cars discreetly parked across the lot.

They walked into the empty school, their feet echoing.

Outside another car door slammed. Mr. Jefferson, bringing Lethe and Rochelle.

It was 7:30. School didn't start until 8:00.

Leave, leave, Eddie thought at his father, who stood so solemnly at his side.

As if he had heard Eddie's thought, Reverend Russell patted Lakeesha on the shoulder and walked away without a word.

The four black students paused in the silent hall and looked at each other.

"Well, here goes!" said Rochelle.

Eddie craned his head to see his father's car drive away. Then he dropped his gym bag to the floor and unzipped it. He pulled out his purple-and-white Douglass letter jacket and put it on.

"Oh, no! You can't wear that here!" said Lakeesha.

Rochelle grinned. "Oh, boy, you going to stir up some hornets you wear that."

Eddie moved his shoulders, settling the jacket just like he wanted it.

Lethe reached out and touched one of the raised white D's that, along with stars, chevrons, and shining metal pins, adorned the jacket.

"Eddie Russell, football star, track star, basketball star, baseball star," she said.

Eddie gave her a crooked smile. "Exactly," he said.

"Barbaric, but effective." Lethe grinned back at him.

In a tight group, they walked Lakeesha to the door of her homeroom as a few white students began sifting into the building. Eddie felt a pang as his sister crept into the room. She looked about three feet tall. Eddie tried to grin at her, but she wouldn't look up.

The white teacher looked toward them, not quite at them.

"That will be your desk." She pointed to the far end of the front row.

Lakeesha sank into the wooden chair.

Eddie tried again to catch Mouse's eye, but they were locked onto her hands. He wanted to go in and shake her for being so scared, he wanted to yell at the teacher for scaring her. Instead he turned and hurried after Rochelle and Lethe. He felt like he'd felt when he and his father had dropped off a sick puppy at the vet's, knowing the vet would put it to sleep. A horrible guilty feeling of relief under the pain.

*   *   *   *

After homeroom, Nancy darted into the girls' bathroom. She twirled in front of the mirror, admiring the flare of her royal-blue summer cheerleading skirt with gold inside the pleats. She hopped to one side and kicked, looking over her shoulder at the snarling lion on the back of the matching blue gabardine vest. The Peter Pan collar of her white blouse was crisp. Her red-gold hair flipped with her twirls, held back by a gold headband. Her blue eyes sparkled with excitement. Nancy loved the first day of school.

The door flew open, and April Rawlins came in, clutching a heavy load of books.

"Hi," April said.

"Hi! Are you in English next?"

"Yes. You?"

Nancy nodded, and they smiled at each other. Nancy had been in English and Latin with April since their freshman year. April was a brain, not in Nancy's crowd, but Nancy liked her, admired her, enjoyed her thoughts. They were in the National Honor Society together. Nancy had just squeaked in after a monumental effort in sophomore geometry, helped along by April and Wayne Rogers.

"Taking Latin again?"

Nancy nodded, pleased. April was one of the few people with whom she didn't have to groan and say, "Daddy's *making* me take Latin." Her father had been a classics major before he went to law school and had insisted she take Latin. He'd have made her take Greek if they'd offered it. He'd read her Greek and Roman myths when other children's parents were reading them Little Golden Books. She secretly loved Latin.

Nancy felt oddly guilty as she turned back to the mirror. Her delight in the gold pleats faded a little.

The bell rang. Nancy ran out of the bathroom and nearly collided with Spencer.

"Spencer! Why don't you look where you're going?"

"You ran into me, sweetie." Spencer patted her on the head and walked into English class one step ahead of her.

Nancy fell into a seat near the windows. She looked across the highway to the fields behind the big Baptist church. The trees were still dark green, the air hazy. Nancy couldn't wait until it got cold, for the trees to turn, to pull her sweaters out of the closet where they were stored in special cedar-lined boxes.

"Oh, guess what! Wayne Rogers asked me out!" Nancy heard Kathy Perkins, the secretary of the class, talking to Sue Ellen Spears as they sat down behind her.

Like all the girls at Forrest, Kathy was making plans to be just like her parents, just like her older sisters. Go to Ole Miss or UT, pledge a good sorority, get married, have children. Kathy even had a hope chest she filled with china and silver and napkins. Just last weekend at a slumber party all the other girls could talk about was getting married and sitting before roaring fires with perfect boys, eating popcorn. They listened to Johnny Mathis croon love songs.

Nancy's daydreams were different; they all ended up in New York or Paris, but still, in the here and now, her gold pleats made her happy.

When she looked up, Nancy was startled to find herself seated directly behind the Negro boy. *He must be boiling in that football jacket,* she thought. Then she gave a little gasp. The jacket was not blue and gold. It was a glaring purple, covered with white stars and large white D's. *Wow!* she thought. *He must have lettered in every sport in the book.*

She watched his profile for a minute, taking in his smooth dark skin, the tick in his jaw muscle, the expressive dark eyes that smoldered at poor Mrs. Cross.

Then she looked away. It wasn't polite to stare. Looking around she saw another Negro, a girl, sitting on the front row.

*   *   *   *

Eddie kept his back straight and his face turned to the front. The other students poured into the room, laughing, talking. Over and over again, he heard the talk and laughter stop and then start again, lower with a hissing sound to it.

All morning he and Rochelle had gotten the gasps, just like the redheaded cheerleader behind him. He wanted to fling his hands up over his head and squeak, "Oh, my! Oh, my!" to mock their outrage.

He gritted his teeth to stop himself from grinning, or screaming. Rochelle sitting two seats in front of him stared out the window, apparently unconcerned. Her shoulders were tight, though, practically up around her ears.

Spencer fell into a seat next to Eddie. He nodded, and Eddie nodded back before he realized it. Spencer's nod had seemed so normal, but it was the first time that day anyone had acknowledged Eddie's existence.

The bell rang with a harsh buzzing right over their heads. Eddie winced.

"Good morning, class and welcome back to school," Mrs. Cross said when the last reverberations faded.

Lost in his thoughts about Spencer's nod, Eddie barely heard a word Mrs. Cross said.

Eddie noticed Spencer tapping his foot impatiently as Mrs. Cross droned on about assemblies and report cards. Spencer drew a halfback pass play on a page in his notebook—x's furiously charging through hapless o's. Eddie almost smiled. He recognized the play.

"Here are your English textbooks. Please sign your names in the front," Miss Cross warbled.

Eddie took the textbook that was passed to him and wrote his name carefully on the list pasted in the front. *Adventures in Literature.* Only one other name was on the list before Eddie's. He flipped through the pages. The books at Douglass fell apart, and the lists ran off the pasted cards and down onto the book covers. A clean smell of coated paper and ink rose from *Adventures in Literature.*

Finally the bell rang again. Eddie tucked his ring binder under his arm and headed slowly out of the building, across the asphalt parking lot, along a path of hard-packed dirt in the dry lawn.

Halfway across the lawn, he heard a high voice shout his name. He stopped, smiling to himself and turned around. Townsend bore down on him like a wildcat.

He stopped about six inches from Eddie and prodded his shoulder with a stiff index finger. "What do you think you're doing wearing that thing?" He shoved Eddie again, with his whole hand this time, but Eddie stood like a rock.

"This?" Eddie asked, innocently. "It's my nigger-school jacket."

He turned and walked into the shop building, leaving Townsend sputtering behind him. He tramped up a narrow flight of stairs and into a big room. Faces turned toward him, all boys.

Spencer was intently running his ink pen into a hole drilled into the long wooden table.

Eddie saw a couple of boys jab each other with their elbows and jerk their heads at him. Their eyes narrowed.

One thin, ferret-faced boy with tattoos on both forearms scratched his cheek and curled his lip.

"You better take that jacket off, boy," he said. Then he spat on the floor.

"Mr. Dozier!" A loud voice made them all jump. A short, round man with a huge red face and impossibly black hair stood in the doorway. "Leonard Dozier, I see that it is my misfortune to have you again in my class and that your manners have not improved over the summer. You will go into the washroom and bring back paper towels sufficient to clean up the mess you have made on the floor of my shop."

Len scowled, never taking his eyes off Eddie.

"Go, sir!" bellowed the teacher, his red cheeks shaking.

Len Dozier reluctantly slid off his stool. He kept his eyes locked on Eddie's as he swaggered out of the room, his thin shoulders twitching. When he disappeared into the hallway, they all heard him begin to whistle.

"Now, young men, we won't wait for Mr. Dozier. I am Mr. Young, your shop instructor. This six weeks we will begin a cabinetry project. We will not finish it this six weeks, of course. We will aim to finish this project by Christmas. By that time, if we are lucky and you young men show even a remote modicum of effort, you should have a nice piece of furniture."

Not a flicker of expression passed across Eddie's face, but inside he smiled. He would dearly love to give his Mama a nice bookcase for Christmas. She'd wanted one for so long.

✳   ✳   ✳   ✳

Nancy and the other girls in second-period gym class groaned. They huddled under the blazing sun by the cinder track behind the elementary school.

"You're not serious, Miss Thoreau," said Cindy Yoder, one of the other junior cheerleaders. "It's the first day of school. We're not in shape!"

"This is how you will get in shape, Cindy," said Miss Thoreau, a short woman built like a fireplug. "Get out there and start your mile. It's only four times around."

"Four times!" the class squealed in unison.

Nancy felt Rochelle bouncing from one foot to the other in the back of the group. The girls jogged miserably onto the track in their white gym short and snapped-front white shirts, white bobby socks and white sneakers. Groaning and giggling they began the long trek to the first turn, where a big tree by the side of the track cast some shade.

Rochelle started to run, a long, reaching stride that effortlessly covered the ground. She passed Nancy and the other girls at the first turn. She passed them again at the point of the far turn, their first lap, and her second. Sally punched Nancy and pointed at Rochelle, open amazement on her face. Nancy wiped the sweat off her forehead. She could have gone faster herself, but didn't want to leave Sally behind. Sally "ran like a girl," her legs flipping out to the side every step she took.

By the time they were back in the shade and beginning their second lap, Rochelle was again at the far turn and coming around to start her third. She finished her fourth lap and left the track as they started their third lap.

"My, my, my," said Miss Thoreau, loudly enough for the whole group of barely jogging girls to hear. "A girl who is actually in condition on the first day of school. In fact, I think these girls couldn't match you on the last day of school, no matter what torture I put them through."

"I love to run." Rochelle bent over and stretched her legs, breathing hard and sweating.

"Good girl. We'll get along," Miss Thoreau said. "Why don't you head back and get dressed. That's all we're doing today."

When Nancy and the other girls limped, groaning, back into the gym dressing room, the shower was hissing. They all looked at each other, then gasped when Rochelle stepped out of the shower, completely naked.

Rochelle laughed. "What's the matter? Ain't y'all never seen a black ass before?" She grabbed a towel and wrapped it around her wet body, heading for her locker.

Nancy laughed. The other girls all spun around and glared at her.

"What? It's funny!"

"We don't talk like that. It's vulgar," said Kathy Perkins.

"It's just that we never take showers, hardly," Sally explained to Rochelle's back.

"Don't take showers?" Rochelle turned to them in amazement. "And y'all think we're dirty!"

Sally turned bright red. "I meant not in P.E."

"Well, don't y'all sweat?"

Nancy laughed again. "You surely noticed that *we* all try *not* to sweat in P.E."

Everyone laughed. They headed to their lockers for their clothes, giggling and talking, washing their faces and hands, fluffing their hair, reapplying their makeup, trying to dress without revealing an inch of bare flesh, taking covert dabs at their armpits with Stridex pads and damp towels. Looking sideways at Rochelle and then at each other, passing a message, "Just ignore the colored girl." It's what Nancy herself had intended to do, but somehow the mean little glances made her mad.

*   *   *   *

As the bell rang, Mr. Young put his hand on Eddie's shoulder, holding him down as the rest of the boys jumped and rushed out.

"Mr. Russell, a word of advice."

Eddie looked up at him, his eyebrows raised.

"I would remove the alien athletic jacket before Coach Ezell sees it."

Eddie looked into Mr. Young's eyes and saw nothing but concern. "But I'm trying to make a point."

"And what is that point, if I might ask?"

"I'm more than just black."

"Yes, sir, young man. I begin to suspect you are."

Eddie grinned. "But maybe I've made the point. Enough for today, anyway?"

Mr. Young laughed. "Yes, sir. Discretion may truly be the better part of valor in this case."

Slowly, Eddie took off the jacket and tucked it into his gym bag.

*   *   *   *

At lunch they met at the door of the cafeteria, Eddie arriving with Rochelle. A blast of noise from inside assailed them. Shrill voices, loud laughter, banging of trays, clattering of dishes and silverware. The sharp smell of vegetable soup drifted out into the hall where they stood.

"Well, come on," said Rochelle and marched in through the swinging screened doors.

Lethe, clutching her geometry book under her arm, pushed her glasses up on her nose and followed. Lakeesha came behind, as close to Lethe's side as she could get. Eddie followed them closely, feeling like a German shepherd guarding a flock.

A group of girls at the Coke machines just inside the door, stopped and glanced at them and then quickly looked away. A little blond girl pushed down the handle of the machine, and the Coke bottle fell down into the slot with a clatter.

They stepped farther into the cafeteria. The big room was full, except for a line of pale wooden tables just inside the door. A few teachers sat at the end of it.

"Let's sit here," Lakeesha said.

Lethe promptly put her geometry book down. "I'm not hungry." She opened the book and began to read, her lips moving silently. Only Lethe could actually read geometry, Eddie thought.

Rochelle rolled her eyes and grabbed Lakeesha's arm. "Come on."

She marched Lakeesha across the room, Eddie close behind, through a sea of noise that ebbed briefly as they passed, then into the line, where a small space magically opened up on either side of them. Eddie looked up and saw a black woman carrying a metal tray of rolls. Their eyes met briefly with a flash of sympathy. Then they quickly looked away from each other.

Rochelle grabbed a plate of gelatinous roast beef and green beans off the glass counter top. Lakeesha followed her lead. Eddie made a show of considering what to get but hardly saw what ended up on his tray. They pushed their trays to the end of the line. A white-haired woman regarded them with hard agate-green eyes. She spat out the amount they owed and carefully took their money without touching their hands.

They carried their trays back to the empty seats at the far end of the teachers' tables.

"Whew!" said Rochelle. "Glad that's over with. Never have to do it for the first time again." She pushed a carton of milk and a roll toward Lethe, who opened the milk and drank it without looking up from her book.

"Hey, girl, you going to lose weight going to school here." Rochelle laughed. Lethe smiled very slightly.

"How can you laugh?" Lakeesha asked.

"Got to keep your sense of humor, Mouse," Eddie said.

He looked out across the cafeteria and despite himself his eyes widened. Coach Ezell was coming toward him, practically at a run, his eyes blazing. Then Coach caught himself, stopped and eyes narrowing, looked closely at Eddie. Eddie swallowed a yelp of laughter. So, he'd heard about the jacket.

Slowly Coach Ezell approached them. Eddie was grateful for the girls' presence. Ezell wouldn't be such a bastard in front of them.

"Russell!"

"Sir?"

"Got a pep rally this afternoon."

"Yes, sir?"

"Come by the gym before we go in. I got your jacket for you."

"Yes, sir."

Ezell turned and hurried out. All three girls turned admiring eyes on Eddie. He allowed himself a small smile.

"Oh, boy, Eddie. I didn't think it would work, but you sure had his number," Rochelle said.

CHAPTER 5

▼

THE CONTENT
OF THEIR
CHARACTER

The next night Forrest played its first home game. From the field where the team was doing stretches, Eddie watched his parents proceed down the cinder track and up the concrete steps into the nearly empty stadium. Mama had a Forrest blue-and-gold ribbon pinned to a big yellow chrysanthemum on her navy blue dress. They took seats on the 50-yard line, two rows back.

Lakeesha, Rochelle and Clifford came in a few feet behind Eddie's parents. Trying not to let Coach Ezell notice him looking, Eddie watched them climb the stands to seats high up on the back row, right under the tiny enclosed press box, where the announcer and the prep sports reporters for the *Commercial Appeal* and the *Press-Scimitar* sat.

As he watched, Eddie realized that right this minute, Vernell was five miles away on the Douglass field, starting at quarterback for the first time. He'd be handing off to Cordray Leonard, who'd taken

Eddie's spot at running back. Eddie closed his eyes and did his jumping jacks, one-two, one-two, one-two.

Coach blew his whistle. The team stopped their jumping jacks and
went to the sidelines in a disorganized huddle. Eddie leaned his back
against the fence and turned his head to watch the crowd coming into
the stadium. Adults and students alike were avoiding the three or four
seats on all sides of his parents.

"This school is just not the same with these colored children."
Eddie jumped at the sound of a sharp female voice. He turned his
head a little further and saw Mrs. Beavers, the Latin teacher who also
happened to be his home-room teacher, passing behind the fence
with a group of other teachers.

"Marion," said Mr. Young. "If you persist in predicting doom, you
will start a stampede."

"Next year there'll be more, and then more and more." Mrs. Beavers turned a withering look on Mr. Young, then saw Eddie standing
on the other side of the fence. She hurried on, a spot of dark red on
each check, and the others followed.

Nancy Martin stood just on the other side of the fence, closer to
the teachers than Eddie was. Her face, too, was mottled with red.
Their eyes met. He turned around with a shrug, expressionless.

A cheer started up behind him.

> *Two bits, four bits*
> *Six bits, a dollar,*
> *All for For-rest*
> *Stand up and holler!"*

Eddie stayed on the bench the whole night, fists clenched, breath
tight in his chest. He moved with every play, his body jerking, tensing, relaxing. He jumped to his feet at the right times, but unlike his
teammates, he never made a sound.

Larry "Touchdown" Townsend threw pass after pass and handed
the ball off desperately to Bobby Davidson. Eddie knew how much

better he was than Bobby. The white boy didn't have his leg strength, or his will. But Coach Ezell would play Bobby, and that was all that mattered.

Nothing worked for Forrest that night. The final score was 14-0.

For the next month, nothing worked. Forrest lost three of the four games, and Eddie stayed on the bench.

*　　　*　　　*　　　*

"Go get your sister, Eddie. She's got to eat her breakfast."

Eddie got up reluctantly, holding a biscuit. Uncle Rayburn looked up from his eggs. Eddie went out to the porch, yanked back the curtains to Lakeesha's room and rattled them loudly.

"Come on, Keesha. Come get your breakfast." Sometimes when he wanted to be especially nice to Lakeesha he called her Keesha instead of Mouse.

Lakeesha didn't turn around.

"Look at her!" She pointed at the newspaper clipping that Mr. Reed had given her so many months ago. Lakeesha had taped the photograph of Diane Nelson to the side of her mirror. "A woman that beautiful can do anything she wants."

"True, you're right, I get it. Now let's go!"

Lakeesha turned around. "Eddie, I hate that school. I hate everything about it. I hate the people. I hate the classes. I even hate the floor. I know the places where the floor tiles don't match, like outside English class. There's a green one there instead of black and white."

"Stop looking at the floor, then."

She wasn't listening. "No one ever speaks to me, no one looks at me, except sort of sideways. It's like I'm not there. Except in gym, that Kinsey Mackay, her and her friends, they go 'Snowflake, snowflake, snowflake' at me. She's so mean."

Eddie sucked in a deep breath. *Stop whining*, he thought. *Stop being such a victim*. When he opened his eyes again, he was under control, and looking at a pile of sweaters on Lakeesha's bed.

"What's all that?" he asked.

Lakeesha didn't turn around. "Nancy Martin's sweaters. I'm giving them all to Etta Lee."

Eddie could hear Mama in the kitchen, singing as she fried their eggs, but Uncle Rayburn had followed him out to the porch and now looked over his shoulder into Keesha's room.

"Why you looking like a noodle's been cooked too long?" he asked.

Eddie looked back, scowling, but Uncle Rayburn hooked his long fingers into the lapels of his tan suit and scowled right back at him with a lot of laughter in his light brown eyes. He was Mama's brother and about as different from their father as it was possible to be. He lived next door and everyone in the neighborhood called him "uncle" whether they were related to him or not.

"I don't know, Uncle Rayburn," Lakeesha said.

Uncle Rayburn adjusted his broad-brimmed white hat and looked down at her, his loose lower lip stuck out and his eyes squinted.

"Girl, you got no reason to go drooping around. You hold your head up!" He threw back his own head and nodded it vigorously once or twice. "Hold your head up! I ain't never gone looking for trouble, but I ain't never bowed my head to no man, no sir, no white man, no black man either."

Lakeesha lifted her chin high, her lips trembling, looking around out of the corners of her eyes.

Eddie laughed. "Hey, Mouse! That's not getting it."

"No, no, no, not like that." Uncle Rayburn grabbed Lakeesha's shoulders and pushed them back. "Stand up straight, pull your shoulders back and hold your head high, every day, every minute of every day. You somebody, Lakeesha. Don't you forget it."

*   *   *   *

Sally's car honked outside in the Martin's gravel driveway. Nancy raced out of her bedroom, down the stairs, then skidded across the rug on the polished floor of the front hall.

"Why does that girl come by here every morning making such a God-awful racket?" Nancy's father looked up over the tops of his glasses, a cup of coffee in his hand, a gardening catalog opened to the iris section on the table in front of him.

"Sally is very nice to give Nancy a ride to school, dear." Her mother, still in her navy-blue robe, examined a glass for spots. Hattie looked around from the stove, where bacon sizzled in a skillet.

"Dad, if you'd just give me a car for Christmas, I could give Sally a ride to school every day, and then you wouldn't have to listen to her honking."

"Oh, no, little missy. The last time I let you use my car, you put a hundred miles on it."

"A hundred miles! What on earth! Where in the world did you go?" her mother yelped.

"I don't know." Nancy grabbed a biscuit from a tray next to Hattie. "I was just driving around."

"But—"

"Cars should also record the top speed reached on the last trip," her father said, turning a page.

Sally honked again.

"I've got to go."

Her mother turned back to an array of china and silver she would use for her bridge club that afternoon. Nancy tore open the biscuit, shoved a piece of bacon inside it, kissed her mother, waved at Hattie and her father, and bolted out the door.

"I just don't think I can stand it anymore," Sally said as Nancy slid into the car seat and slammed the door. "We've got to start winning games! We've lost four in a row now."

"We're jinxed."

"I know exactly what our jinx is."

"He's not even playing. How could he be the jinx?"

"I don't care. He's a jinx."

"He's a jinx," Nancy chanted and clapped her hands, *clap clap.*

"He's a jinx," Sally responded, hitting the horn twice.

"He's a J-I-N-K-S, yes," Nancy chanted.

"That's not how you spell jinx, you idiot," Sally screamed, laughing so hard the car swerved dangerously.

"I don't care. It's got to sound right, like Miss Cross says in English class; it's got to sca-a-a-a-n."

*   *   *   *

When he got to school, Eddie slammed the locker room door open with his shoulder, marching down the concrete aisle toward his locker to drop off his gym bag, circling to get around Spencer, whose bulk blocked most of the narrow passage.

Spencer gazed fondly at the festoons of ribbons and medals and photos of his football heroes that lined the inside of his locker. Eddie watched out of the corner of his eyes as Spencer ran his finger over the raised gold F for Forrest High on his shiny blue jacket. Eddie stifled a smile and threw his bag into his locker with a clang.

Then his thoughts fell back into their well-worn groove. *Why won't Coach play me? So what if I'm black? I'm good. He knows it.*

Every evening when practice ended, Coach made Eddie run extra laps. But for all the extra conditioning, Eddie had been sitting on the bench through every game. Eddie had stopped tensing with every play. He never jumped up to cheer anymore. He just sat there, still playing each down in his head and heart.

Eddie and Spencer left the gym at the same time and walked next to each other without speaking through the warren of shop buildings reeking with the smell of glues and solvents. As they passed the science building and started toward the Old Building, the silence between them stretched uncomfortably, yet Eddie couldn't find a way either to hurry up or slow down so they could walk apart.

"So, what do you think of the game tonight?" Spencer asked finally.

Eddie looked at him, surprised. "It'll be tough. Forrest should win though. You're a better team. You should have won all the games this year."

Spencer looked at Eddie, his eyes hurt. "We! We're a good team."

Eddie looked at Spencer but said nothing. His mind did a little flip as he realized he had never once thought of the Forrest team as "we." That was still Douglass. When he talked to Vernell, he always asked how "we" were doing.

"Hi, Spence."

Both boys jumped at the voice. Nancy Martin blocked their way up the stairs into the New Building, where their home room was.

"Hello, little person," said Spencer.

"Are you going to buy a ribbon?" She held out two blue-and-gold ribbons that said "Maul Morristown." She pushed one of them at Eddie and looked right at him. He couldn't pretend she wasn't talking to him as well as Spencer.

Eddie reached into his pocket, hooked out a coin and handed it to Nancy, avoiding her eyes. *Don't so much as look...*he thought. She gave him a ribbon.

"See you tonight, Mack." Nancy grinned up at Spencer. Eddie looked at her sideways, puzzled, but Spencer just rolled his eyes.

Nancy moved aside, and Eddie and Spencer moved on down the hall.

"I think she likes you, man," said Eddie, and then stopped suddenly when he realized he'd mentioned a white girl to a white man. Not only that. He'd spoken about her *liking* somebody.

"Oh, hell, no. The girls just tease me, is all." Spencer paused, waited for Eddie to start walking again, and they continued down the hall to home room. "They have ever since grade school. She's probably still got a crush on that jerk Townsend. They went out last year."

They looked back over their shoulders. Sure enough, Nancy was giggling with Sally, both of them looking at Spencer.

Townsend, huh? Eddie thought.

*   *   *   *

That night, the team rode home on the bus from Morristown, sullen and dejected. They had lost again. Eddie had not played. He sat in the front seat of the bus, locked inside his head, trying to think of nothing, right behind the black driver. Two seats separated him from Coach Ezell, who sat alone. The team huddled as far into the back of the bus as they could cram. Even after losing, they still laughed and pushed at each other. Eddie watched the road over the driver's shoulder, white lines on black asphalt, clicking by, like his junior year football season.

CHAPTER 6

▼

WINNERS WE MUST BE

On a glorious Friday in early October, Nancy nervously shook her pom-poms outside the boys' gym. Missy Bond, the cheerleading captain, marched up and down the line, very much the senior.

"Stop that giggling," she barked at them, her freckled face white with tension.

Since no one was giggling, that made Cindy, the other junior cheerleader, giggle. Sally and Nancy both turned to her and shook their pom-poms in her face, a frenzy of gold.

"Stop it!" Missy screamed. "It's time to go!"

They put their hands on their hips, pom-poms ready. Nancy couldn't look at Sally because if she did she'd start laughing again. As it was, her shoulders kept jerking with suppressed giggles. They were wearing their winter uniforms for the first time that day, royal blue skirts and sweaters with gold lions on the back. Sweater weather at last. Nancy loved October.

Missy listened for a cue from the band, which had already marched in and taken its place in the bleachers. The band struck up the school fight song, "On, Forrest." A roar from the doors of the gym wrapped around them.

Missy beat her pom-poms together three times and said, "Okay, let's go!"

They ran into the gym behind her, clapping their pom-poms in time to the music. They formed two lines and ran into place, half the squad facing each side of the gym, which was packed to the rafters. Everyone sang lustily:

> *On For-rest, on For-rest*
> *On to victory,*
> *Take the ball right down the field*
> *For winners we must be,*

"Rah, Rah, Rah," shook the building, and the football team ran in the doors and onto the gym floor.

Was it her imagination or did the cheers from the crowd falter as the team spread out across the middle of the gym floor? Did a sour note creep into the band's playing? Nancy's moment of hesitation threw the cheerleaders a beat off.

Missy beat her pom-poms together. The cheerleaders caught her beat, and then they were all back in synch. The cheering rose again, loud, certainly loud, but not like earlier in the year when the gym shook with the noise. Nancy's head ached.

Jump, jump, kick, shake. Turn, jump, jump, kick, shake, Nancy counted the steps out in her head. The band toiled in brazen fury, tubas and trombones and the beat, beat, beat of the drums. They slid into a new song:

> *Oh, they call him Mr. Touchdown.*
> *Oh, yes, they call him Mr. T.*
> *He can run and he can throw.*
> *Give him the ball,*
> *And just look at him go!*

Jump, jump, kick, shake. Nancy thought.

"Not much energy in this bunch," Nancy whispered to Sally as they passed each other.

"Nope," Sally whispered back.

> *So give a great big cheer*
> *For the hero of the year.*
> *Mr. Touchdown, Forrest H.S.*

They gave their gold pom-poms a last shake. Losing teams never inspired much enthusiasm, especially for fans used to winning every game. And so far Forrest had lost every game but one. The crowd gave a last bellow, and the pep rally was over. Everyone began drifting to class.

"Gosh!" said Missy. "This used to be fun." She flounced off.

The football team in their blue-and-gold jackets drifted apart, spiraling away from the one black face among them.

Larry Townsend dropped back and pushed his way in between Nancy and Sally, draping a long arm around each of them. "So, I hear you got a new cheer, something about a J-I-N-K-S."

"Yes." Nancy twisted away and clapped derisively at Larry. "It's you!"

Sally must have told the football players about the J-I-N-K-S cheer, Nancy thought. *Can't keep her big mouth shut.*

Nancy marched away, Sally beside her. She felt Larry watching her but didn't look back.

"Why does he keep after you like that?"

"He's a jerk." Nancy flipped her sweaty red-gold hair off her neck and waved a hand in front of her hot face. "He called twelve times last night. Daddy's getting ready to change our number if he doesn't stop."

Nancy watched Kathy Perkins and Wayne Rogers walking hand-in-hand in front of them. She still felt a little bad that he'd never asked her out. Not that she would have gone, but still.

Wayne glanced back at them, a shy smile on his serious face. Kathy spoke, and Wayne leaned toward her, his glasses slipping down his nose.

"Aren't they just the two little sweeties?" Nancy whispered to Sally. Sally giggled.

Near the shop buildings, they passed a group of boys loitering by the smoking club. Boys who had signed permission from their parents could smoke in this space between the science building and the carpentry shop, a circle of hard-packed brown dirt and scrubby trees.

The boys were well outside the smoking club, but they were smoking nonetheless and laughing. Nancy saw one of the Negro girls ahead of them, hurrying past the boys. She heard ugly laughter, and the Negro girl began walking so fast she almost ran. Nancy sped up to keep her in sight.

"Why are you going so fast?" Sally panted.

Nancy saw Len Dozier flip a cigarette toward the Negro girl. "Catch, nigger," he said.

The cigarette slithered down the girl's arm. She beat the sparks off her sweater and then ran for a few steps. Nancy turned to glare at Len, but as she opened her mouth to say something, she remembered that people like her didn't speak to people like him. She closed her mouth and turned around in time to see the girl trip and fall, her hands in the dust.

Outside the smoking club, boys laughed uproariously. "The nigger bitch goes down!" one of them jeered.

Surrounded by titters of laughter, Nancy pushed toward the girl but couldn't get through the crowd. Crouching down, Nancy saw hurrying legs, legs in pants and loafers, white socks and loafers, legs in hose and flats. Then she saw a foot stamp on an outstretched dark hand. Sally yanked at Nancy's arm, pulling her up.

A chant started up in the smoking club as the Negro girl struggled to her feet.

Two, four, six, eight,
We don't want to integrate,
Five, four, three, two,
Send them back to Tugaloo.

Then they began to spit in her direction.

The girl ran, blood beginning to stain her white ankle socks.

Nancy rounded on the smoking club, Sally still pulling desperately at her sleeve. "Nancy, stop, stop."

Nancy snatched her arm away and glared at Sally. "What's the matter with you?" she asked, then she turned back to the grinning smoking club.

"You are scum!" she said.

Dozier at the forefront smiled and pulled another cigarette out of his pack, flipped open his Zippo lighter and struck a flame to the tip. Nancy took a step toward him. Dozier's smile faded. The other boys peeled off and swaggered toward the shop building.

Nancy felt Sally fluttering behind her. *If she grabs me again, I'll kill her,* she thought, her eyes still on Dozier. She took another step. Dozier's eyes dropped; he took a step back. Then he turned, laughed and walked away.

Nancy turned back to Sally, her teeth clenched, but satisfied.

"What on earth was that all about, Nancy? Have you gone crazy? You don't want to mess with those boys."

They were nearly alone on the lawn between the Old Building and the shops. The home-room bell rang.

"I don't understand you at all." Nancy started to walk. She couldn't look at Sally. "How could you just stand there and not do something?" she asked.

Sally didn't answer. They walked into the Old Building in silence and split at the top of the stairs to go into their separate home rooms.

*   *   *   *

As Eddie left home room, someone passing him hissed, "We got your sister."

Eddie froze in the hallway. Had he heard right? Students poured around him, yelling, laughing. He didn't look up.

He marched down the hall into Lakeesha's home room and went up to Mrs. Sanders, who moved to put the desk between them.

"Where's my sister?" he asked quietly.

"In the nurse's office," Mrs. Sanders didn't quite look at him. "She cut her knees."

Eddie's hands clenched.

"She's perfectly all right," Mrs. Sanders said.

Eddie looked at the clock on the wall, ignoring Mrs. Sanders. He had English class in three minutes. He ran down the hall to the nurse's office. She looked up in alarm when the door banged open.

"Where's my sister?" he asked.

"She's gone. She just cut her knees a little bit. She's fine," the nurse said.

Eddie couldn't remember what class Lakeesha had first period. He glanced at the clock on the nurse's wall. One minute to English class, but Eddie wasn't going to go to English class.

Everything came to a point in his mind, all the past months' frustration and pain and constant tension, every one of Mouse's whines, every white line on the highways home from games, every cold smile on his father's face when he bent his head at the supper table to pray for strength.

He stood in the middle of the hall, his eyes on the floor. He saw a green tile in the middle of all the black and white ones. *That's the one. Lakeesha's tile*, he thought.

He raised his head, marched out of the building, across the parking lot and into the gym. When he got to the door to Coach's office, he didn't hesitate. The door banged open and Coach Ezell almost jumped to his feet in alarm and then sank back down with a sour smile on his face.

"Coach, I have to talk to you."

Coach ran his hand over his dark crew cut. His flat nose looked like it had been badly broken at some point. His dark, thick eyebrows nearly met over his nose, contrasting strangely with his light blue eyes.

Eddie suddenly remembered a story he'd heard just that week. Coach Ezell had once given an entire gym class of more than sixty boys three licks each, for betting on coin tosses, one hundred and eighty strokes of his paddle against their young backsides without pausing to take a break. Must have been one of his finest hours, Eddie thought.

"You're supposed to be in class."

"I have to talk to you."

Coach pointed at a chair. "So talk."

"I want to quit."

Coach studied him in silence for a moment, then rolled his finger in the air, indicating, "Go on."

"Somebody must have pushed my sister down. She cut her knees and somebody said to me, 'We got your sister.' She's miserable here. She never wanted to do this. She's a mouse, just a little, gentle mouse. I'm doing nothing here. You won't play me, and we've only got two more games. I want to go back to Douglass. At least I'll get some playing time. A lot depends on that. I need a scholarship. I need to play. If I'm just sitting on a bench, what am I doing here?"

Coach got up and walked around closer to Eddie, half sat on the desk.

"Damned if I know."

They stared at each other for a few seconds, then both looked away.

"I don't care how you treat me," Eddie said, looking at their reflection in the glass of the trophy case. "I'm in better shape than I've ever been because of what you've done to me. I just want to play. There's no point my being here and putting up with all this and my sister putting up with it if I don't get to play."

"That's mighty noble of you Russell. Your sister gets hurt and you come in here saying, 'Play me, or I quit.' Sorry if I can't quite make the connection."

"I can't help that. It's how I feel. I want to quit. There's no point in this if I can't be who I am."

"And if you play, to hell with your sister?"

Eddie stopped cold, shocked. That's just what he'd been saying, wasn't it?

Coach smiled in satisfaction. "So, that's fine with me. Quit. Run back to Douglass. You might not get to start there after all this time, with Coach Frazier always going on about 'team.'" Coach went back around the desk and sat down. "I'll call your father and tell him not to come to this meeting he's asked for with me."

"What meeting?"

"Hell if I know," Coach said. "He made an appointment for 8:30 this morning."

They both looked at the clock. It was 8:27. At that moment, two sharp raps on the door made them jump.

*   *   *   *

Nancy darted into the bathroom, still mad, still seeing that girl's hand and the foot coming down on it. As she turned on the water to wash her hands, she was startled to hear strangled sobbing from inside one of the stalls. She knocked on the door and called, "What's wrong? Who's there?"

"Go away!"

"I'm not going away. What's wrong?"

"Everyone hates me," a hoarse voice whispered.

Nancy bent down and looked under the door. She saw a pair of brown legs in bloodstained white ankle socks and black patent leather strapped flats.

"Everyone doesn't hate you."

Behind the green metal door, the stifled sobs continued.

"I don't hate you."

Unabated sobs and a long gasping breath.

"I don't know what to say. I don't know how to talk to you," Nancy whispered.

Scuffling sounds and another gasp. Nancy bent down again and saw the girl's skirt, realized she must be folding herself into the very back of the stall.

"Wait here." Nancy bolted out of the girls' bathroom, realizing how absurd her comment had been. That girl definitely was not going anywhere.

She stood in the alcove outside the bathroom. The smell of the red powder the janitors threw down before they swept stung her nose. She had to get help, but who could she find that wouldn't hurt the girl's feelings even more?

It occurred to Nancy that she didn't even know the girl's name. She had thought she would never have a reason to learn their names. They were never going to speak to them, right? Not be ugly, just never, ever acknowledge their existence.

Nancy made a sudden decision. She darted down the hall, around the corner and down another short hall to the cosmetology department.

Nancy burst through the door. The room reeked of permanent solution.

"Mrs. Odetts!"

Mrs. Odetts, her glasses at the end of her nose, peered at a student's attempt to wind an older woman's gray hair onto tiny pink rollers. Outside customers came to the Forrest cosmetology department and saved a bundle on their haircuts and permanents.

Mrs. Odetts looked at Nancy over the tops of her glasses.

"Yes, Nancy?"

Nancy instantly felt rumpled under that discerning eye, tugged her perfectly smooth sweater down and stood up straighter.

"Can I speak to you outside for a minute?"

Kinsey Mackay squinted curiously at Nancy, tightening the roller. Nancy knew vaguely who she was, one of the girls with a bad reputation, a girl she never spoke to if she could at all avoid it.

"Ouch!" yelped Kinsey's customer.

"Excuse us for a moment, Mrs. Smith." Mrs. Odetts adjusted her glasses and swept out of the room with Nancy.

"Well, Nancy, what is it?"

Nancy saw Mrs. Smith and Kinsey watching through the half-opened door, their heads cocked at exactly the same angle.

Nancy moved out of their sight and whispered, "One of those kids, you know, the colored kids. She's crying in the bathroom and won't come out."

Mrs. Odetts frowned, then strode down the hall around the corner and into the bathroom, Nancy hurrying in her wake.

"Open the door, dear," said Mrs. Odetts.

"No, no, *no*!" wailed the girl on the other side.

Nancy's chest tightened. Until that moment when Len Dozier had thrown the cigarette, Nancy had not once bothered to think of the Negro students' feelings.

"Nancy, go under the door."

Nancy looked at her in astonishment. Mrs. Odetts pointed at the floor. Nancy shook her head once, then, got down on the floor, crawled under the door and stood up inside the stall.

The Negro girl crouched in a ball against the back wall.

"Please don't cry." Nancy opened the stall door, feeling like a traitor.

"Come out, dear," said Mrs. Odetts. Nancy looked at her in surprise. She'd never thought a tone that gentle could come out of no-nonsense Mrs. Odetts.

At that moment the door to the bathroom banged open. Mrs. Smith waddled in on a waft of permanent solution, her pink-flowered wrap billowing. Nancy realized with a shock that it was Spencer's mother. She hadn't recognized her in rollers and a beauty-shop cape.

Mrs. Smith took one look at the girl, went right into the stall, and put her arms around her. "Don't you cry, honey. What's wrong?"

The girl threw her arms around Mrs. Smith's soft neck and wept.

Mrs. Smith shook her pink-rollered head. "I guess someone's been ugly to this poor little thing. I don't know why people are making such a fuss about a few black children going to a new school."

"Nancy, go outside and make sure no one else comes in," Mrs. Odetts said. "Sandra and I will handle this."

Mrs. Odetts, patted the sobbing girl's back. Nancy turned and saw Kinsey's malicious face peeking in the door.

"What's wrong with little Snowflake?" Kinsey hissed.

"Get out!"

"My aren't we all the nigger-lovers today."

Nancy pushed past Kinsey, who smirked and swished away back down the hall.

Nancy stood guard outside the bathroom. The bell rang, and students surged through the hallways to third period.

"Sorry, this bathroom's flooded," Nancy said over and over again as girls came to the door. "They're cleaning it up now."

*   *   *   *

"So, your boy wants to quit, Reverend," said Coach, leaning back in his chair. The chair banged into the glass of a dusty trophy case.

Eddie met his father's eyes. "Dad," he said. "I need to talk to you."

His father looked slightly off-balance but hid it well. Without speaking to Eddie, Reverend Russell looked around the room, saw a folding chair, opened it and sat down, a yellow Visitor badge neatly clipped to his lapel.

"Dad, it's about Lakeesha."

Reverend Russell held up his hand. Eddie braced for a lecture, but his father spoke only to Coach.

"Coach Ezell, what do you expect of your players?"

"Winning."

"What do you hope they will do after they leave Forrest?"

"Play college ball and remember what I taught 'em."

Reverend Russell stood and placed a small sheaf of newspaper clippings on Coach's desk.

Coach flipped them with one finger. "What's this?"

"Negro boys are playing college football, Coach Ezell. Negroes are playing professional football. I predict that within a year, sir, they will be playing in the Southeast Conference. You're missing a chance to realize your ambitions if you don't play my son."

Coach picked up one of the clippings and slowly read it, then put it down and said, "That will never happen. Nigras will never play in the SEC."

Reverend Russell raised his eyebrows at the word "nigra," which was how white people of Coach Ezell's type now said "nigger," and thought they were being polite.

Then Reverend Russell nodded to himself and reached across the desk to hand the coach a letter. Coach Ezell took the letter out of its envelope and scanned it. His face turned red, and he slammed his fist on the desk.

"I'm sorry, Mr. Ezell, but you play my son or you risk a lawsuit. And, as you see, your school superintendent would prefer not to take that risk."

Coach Ezell looked down at his hands for a long moment, then he turned to Eddie.

"I'll play you once, Russell, to get these bureaucrats off my back. But you'll have to prove something to me if you ever want me to play you again."

Eddie nodded and stood up. He and his father left Coach's office and walked out into the bright sunlight of late September. They looked at each other.

"What was that all about, Dad?"

"I didn't have anything to do with it. Coach Frazier got so angry that Forrest hasn't played you that he talked to the NAACP. They wrote to the County School Superintendent. The superintendent wrote to me saying he would order Ezell to play you, if I approved it. I've been sitting on this letter for a week. I thought your coach might come to it on his own, but clearly that was an unreasonable expectation."

Eddie bit his lip and frowned. He didn't quite like it—his daddy coming to school to bail him out of his troubles, the NAACP having to step in.

"What's this about you wanting to quit?" his father asked. "What were you doing in Coach Ezell's office? Aren't you supposed to be in class?"

Before Eddie could answer, Coach Ezell stuck his head out the door of the locker room. "Reverend Russell!"

"Yes?"

"Office called to say your girl's there. Better go see what's the matter." He ducked back inside, and banged the door behind him.

*   *   *   *

Mrs. Granger was holding Lakeesha's hand and patting her back when Reverend Russell opened the door to her office, Eddie right behind.

Mrs. Granger shook her curly head at them, her face twisted with sympathy. Lakeesha pulled away from Mrs. Granger and threw herself into her father's arms.

"I want to go back to Douglass," Lakeesha whispered into his black shirt and white clerical collar.

"But daughter, why?"

"It's awful, Daddy. The first thing anyone has said to me at this school is 'nigger-bitch.' And they pitched a cigarette at me and spit at me and chanted at me. I ran and then I fell and cut my knees, and somebody stomped on my hand. They chant 'snowflake, snowflake,' over and over again. But they never speak to me, Daddy, never speak to me at all. They talk to each other, but it's at me. I can't stand it. I want to quit. I never wanted to do this in the first place."

Eddie felt a surge of relief. Mouse was sticking up for herself. Her head came up off her father's chest, her shoulders went back. *Hold your head up!* Eddie thought.

"Why can't we just let things go on the way they've always been? What's wrong with Douglass? What's wrong with separate schools? I never want to see another white person again as long as I live."

"Keesha, dear girl. In Nashville, they put cigarettes out on our people's heads. They poured milk on two young women who were graduates of Mount Holyoke College. They turned fire hoses on children younger than you in Birmingham and blew up little girls at church. They beat our people with ax handles in Selma, and they murdered our people in Mississippi. Surely you can stand a few words."

Lakeesha hung her head. "Why me?" she whispered.

"Would you rather it be someone else? Should someone else take your place? Would it be better for them than for you?"

"No, Daddy."

Yes, it would, Eddie thought. *Mouse is the last person able to stand this.* He couldn't believe his father didn't know it, or didn't care.

Reverend Russell reached out and took Lakeesha's hands, wet with her tears. Lakeesha's head went back down onto her father's chest.

Eddie stood by the door, hands clenched. He caught a look of smug satisfaction on Mrs. Granger's face. She darted a glance at him and the smirk was quickly wiped away and replaced with her usual expression of concern and sympathy. Eddie looked quickly at Lakeesha and saw her freeze, her eyes locked on Mrs. Granger, her mouth open in surprise.

Lakeesha gazed straight into Mrs. Granger's blue eyes, and the blue eyes dropped. Mrs. Granger blushed.

Reverend Russell pulled a white handkerchief out of his pocket and dried Lakeesha's eyes.

"Daddy, I will stay here at Forrest," Lakeesha said, her eyes locked on Mrs. Granger.

"My daughter," Reverend Russell said, and then broke off and gave Lakeesha a hug, patting her back.

"Whatever you decide, Reverend Russell, I think that Lakeesha should go home for the day," Mrs. Granger said.

Reverend Russell nodded.

"I have to go to a meeting downtown, and your mother has gone shopping," he said, still patting Lakeesha's face with the square of white cotton. "I'll have to drop you by the Martins' and you can stay with Hattie. Eddie, you'd better get back to class."

"Perhaps Eddie as well…" Mrs. Granger began.

"My son can return to class," Reverend Russell said.

✳   ✳   ✳   ✳

Nancy pushed open the swinging screen door into the cafeteria and stepped inside. This day just wouldn't stop, even though all she wanted was to go home and try to sort out her feelings. The cafeteria reverberated with loud voices, scraping chairs, the clatter of silverware, the bump of trays. The surge of bodies and smell of hot dogs and baked beans made her a little sick. It was like waking up from a bad dream when everything in the room looks different and strange. Only she couldn't lie back down and close her eyes until everything went back to normal.

Sally was already there, sitting at their usual table with their usual friends. She saw Nancy and waved, but Nancy didn't respond.

Far away at the other end of the cafeteria Nancy saw two black girls sitting at the end of the line of cafeteria tables where the teachers ate. Since the first day, the black students had sat there alone. Even the teachers left them plenty of space.

Nancy started across the cafeteria. She had to talk to them, had to tell them about their friend. They might be worried. They might be able to help.

"I'll be back in a minute," she said as she passed Sally.

When she got to the Negro girls' table, she stood there for a moment. They looked up at her, puzzled and wary.

Nancy took a deep breath and sat down.

The cafeteria bedlam noticeably quieted. Nancy was sure that every person in the lunchroom had gasped in amazement. The hum of conversation and clatter started up again, laced with the unmistakable high buzz of gossip.

Nancy could just imagine what everybody was saying.

"What on earth?"

"Do you see what I see?"

"Is that Nancy Martin eating with the colored girls?"

"Hi, my name's Nancy Martin."

"I know your name," Rochelle said. "From gym glass."

"Yes, and I know yours, Rochelle Perry. But I don't know your friend's name."

"Lethe Jefferson," Lethe said, with a small, tight smile.

"Lethe, the river in the underworld." Her father had taught her the entire geography of the land of death.

"Yes," said Lethe, her smile broader.

"Forgetfulness."

The two girls looked at each other, for a moment sharing a flash of recognition that neither could have quite explained.

"Where's Lakeesha? And Eddie?" Rochelle asked, looking around the cafeteria.

"Actually, I saw Lakeesha," Nancy said. "Is that her name? She had...she...she fell. She cut her knees. I think her Daddy came to get her."

Rochelle and Lethe looked suspiciously at Nancy.

"What are you trying to say? What did they do to Keesha?" Rochelle asked.

"I think she fell, but somebody might have pushed her. I don't know. But that's what I wanted to say. I wanted to apologize. I wanted to say I never really thought about how you all must feel and how mean we've been and how brave you are." Nancy's blue eyes filled with tears.

"Oh, well, you've always been one of the better ones. At least you laugh when I make a joke," Rochelle said glumly.

"But you're funny."

They looked at each other and laughed.

Miss Thoreau passed by just then and slapped Rochelle on the shoulder. "Track stars don't drink Cokes." She lifted the Coke bottle off Rochelle's tray and slammed it down again with a bark of laughter.

CHAPTER 7

▼

STOP! IN THE NAME OF LOVE

Nancy slammed the door of Sally's blue Mustang and stepped back against Hattie's car as Sally tore out of the gravel driveway. She and Sally had been arguing all the way home from school, about Nancy having "noticed" the colored girls.

She jumped in alarm as someone sat up in the back of Hattie's car. When she recognized Lakeesha, Nancy smiled, broadly at first. Then her smile faded at the corners when Lakeesha did not smile back.

"Lakeesha? Is that you? Are you all right? What are you doing in Hattie's car?"

Lakeesha shook her head to wake up. "I was sleeping."

Nancy still looked confused.

"Aunt Hattie's my aunt."

"She is? You're kidding!" Why had no one told her this? It was very embarrassing not to have known that. "Do you want to come in?" Then she stopped. Would her mother like that? She looked at Lakeesha and saw the doubt and skepticism on her face.

"No, no, Aunt Hattie wouldn't like it," Lakeesha said. "She made me stay out here in the car because your mother is having some kind of party."

Nancy frowned. "Well, you want to come out and sit in the swing?"

Lakeesha looked at the white wooden swing hanging from the branch of a pin oak tree that spread across the Martins' back yard.

"Okay." She got out of the car without meeting Nancy's eyes.

"I'll go get us something to drink. Go sit down, I'll be right back." Nancy ran up the back steps onto the porch of the rambling, white frame house. The screen door slammed. Nancy hurried through another door, into the kitchen. She could hear her mother's friends laughing and caught a glimpse of Hattie in the back laundry room, ironing.

She glanced out the window and saw Lakeesha picking her way barefooted across the grass toward the swing, avoiding the prickly balls from the sweet gum trees embedded in the soft ground. She sank down on the swing and set herself slowly swinging, turning her face up toward the sun.

Nancy turned quickly to the ice box, flung it open, grabbed the metal pitcher of lemonade that usually sat on the top shelf and poured two glasses.

As she hurried back outside, a blue jay screamed, and a cardinal answered, saying over and over, "Pretty, pretty, pretty."

The Martins' golden retriever, Blondie, walked behind her, her tail waving, her face laughing. She caught sight of Lakeesha and woofed once, then ambled over and stuck her head in the girl's lap. Lakeesha smiled and tentatively patted her golden head.

Nancy sat on the swing, making it jerk, then handed one of the glasses to Lakeesha. Nancy looked at the etching on her glass, an M with grape leaves. She thought of Hattie washing those glasses in hot water, wiping them with soft white cloths.

"My mother's playing bridge. I got us some lemonade."

Lakeesha looked puzzled. "Bridge?" she asked.

Nancy had a quick image of her mother playing London Bridge Is Falling Down with her friends. She laughed. Lakeesha looked down at her lap.

"Oh, it's a card game," Nancy said, trying to make Lakeesha look up. "Very boring. I laughed because I imagined them in there playing London Bridge."

Lakeesha smiled briefly and tried to push Blondie's heavy head off her leg.

"Stop it, Blondie," Nancy said. "You're going to make her spill her lemonade. Go lie down."

Blondie looked at Nancy, hurt, then flopped onto the grass with a gusty sigh.

The two girls looked at each other.

"I saw Rochelle and Lethe at lunch. They asked where you were. I told them you'd gotten hurt."

Lakeesha winced, looking down at the big pink bandages on her dark knees. Nancy waited for her to say something.

"After the pep rally, some of those boys, you know, at the smoking club, they—"

"I know. I saw it. I was right behind you leaving the pep rally."

Lakeesha leaned back in the swing and closed her eyes. Both girls were silent for a long moment.

"I never thought until today how hard it must be…," Nancy's voice trailed off, and they rocked back and forth in the sun.

"I'm afraid," Lakeesha said after a moment. "I'm afraid all the time, every second of every day. I don't know how I stand it."

Nancy saw Lakeesha's lips quiver. The girl's face was not beautiful. Her hair curled in a fringe on her forehead and lay straight down across the tops and sides of her head, processed to flip at the ends. Her face was thin, her nose flat, her lips full. She was small and dressed in cheap clothes. But when she looked up at Nancy, her eyes were so beautiful and sad that Nancy's own eyes began to sting with tears. She blinked hard.

"I can see why they picked the others," Lakeesha went on. "Lethe's smart and Eddie's an athlete and Rochelle, she's such a, a, a…"

"Personality."

"Yes, exactly. She's so funny and says just what she thinks. People like her and respect her and don't mess with her, at least not too much. But me, they only picked me to go to Forrest because I'm Eddie's sister and Daddy's daughter. I was an afterthought. There's absolutely no point in my being there."

"You're Eddie's sister? I didn't know that."

Lakeesha nodded, swinging.

"Maybe you've got something the others don't. Somehow you made me *feel* for you. I had heard sort of that Lethe was really smart, and I knew myself that Rochelle was funny, and of course, I know that Eddie's a football player. But it hadn't gotten through to me somehow, what you all were doing. I had just completely blocked it out. Do you like Bob Dylan?" Nancy asked.

"No-o-o," Lakeesha said.

Nancy wasn't listening. "All of a sudden today I thought, you all are 'the warriors whose strength is not to fight,' like in that song."

Lakeesha looked at Nancy, her forehead wrinkled, and Nancy felt foolish.

"Who *do* you like?" Nancy asked.

"What?"

"What music? What groups?"

"Well, I like the music in our church. And I like the Temptations, The Drifters, Wilson Pickett, the Supremes."

Nancy spun around, making the swing jump again.

"The Supremes? I just got their new album. Come on, let's go listen to it."

Nancy jumped up, waking up Blondie, who struggled to her feet and stretched out in a bow to the girls.

"Come on!"

"Are you sure it's all right?"

"Sure, we'll just sneak up the back stairs. Mother will never know we're there."

Lakeesha followed Nancy across the yard, across the porch and through the door to the kitchen. It was empty, with something bubbling on blue jets of gas. Nancy tiptoed across the black-and-white tiled floor into a dark room like a closet. Coats, hats, and dog leashes hung from hooks. A narrow staircase led up into darkness. Nancy bolted up the stairs, her feet loud on the wooden stairs. Lakeesha followed lightly, silently.

They reached the upstairs hallway. Nancy opened the door to her room, ran in, reached back, pulled Lakeesha in and slammed the door. Nancy looked down at her hand, holding Lakeesha's hand. She let it go.

Nancy opened her record player, a cubic wooden box. She grabbed The Supremes album and shoved it past the lever on the metal changer. She lifted the arm with a frown of concentration, her lip caught in her teeth, and set the needle down, right at the beginning of...

STOP in the name of love.

The girls looked at each other in delight. Nancy stuck her hand out, palm forward. Lakeesha half-lifted her hand.

They both crossed their hands over their hearts, swaying to the music.

They swayed and sang.

STOP...

Both hands went up and arms went out in unison this time.

The door banged open. Nancy's mother stood in the door, elegant in a pink polished cotton shirtwaist dress, a pearl choker around her neck.

"Nancy Louise, turn down that music! You nearly scared us to death!"

Both girls dropped their outstretched hands. Nancy yanked the needle off the record with a painful scratch.

Her mother's irritated expression changed to a look of surprise when she caught sight of Lakeesha. Her eyes traveled from Lakeesha's head, over her dusty sweater and down to her bare feet.

"Why, Nancy, I didn't know you had company." She couldn't seem to tear her eyes away from Lakeesha's feet.

Hattie appeared in the doorway.

"Lakeesha! Girl, what are you doing up here? I thought I told you to stay in the car. You get on downstairs now. It's time to go home. Here you waists, Nancy." She handed Nancy a pile of freshly ironed blouses and hustled Lakeesha out of the room.

Lakeesha was stiff with embarrassment, but Nancy's mouth twitched at the corners.

"Are you going to the game tonight?" Nancy hurried after Lakeesha, shoving past Hattie to walk beside her.

Lakeesha gave a quick nod. Hattie tried to push at Lakeesha's back, but Nancy moved in her way.

"All the way to Pineville?"

Lakeesha nodded again. Hattie put her hands on both their backs and hurried them down the stairs.

"Then I'll see you there." Nancy chattered away, mindlessly, thinking only of her mother upstairs in all her frosty rudeness. "What are you going to wear? Where are you going to sit? Do you think we'll win?"

Lakeesha barely spoke. Hattie waddled behind them, muttering to herself.

Hours later, at dinner, Nancy was still fuming.

"What was that all about, Mother?"

"What, dear?"

"For your information, that girl, who happens to be Hattie's niece, had a particularly horrible day, and I was just trying to cheer her up. I don't know how many times I've heard you say Hattie is just like one of the family. Well, I just treated Lakeesha like she really was a member of the family." Nancy's voice rose in anger.

Her mother looked at Nancy for a long moment, her prominent blue eyes troubled. She leaned back in her chair.

"I remember once when I was a girl, Nancy. I used to go down to Mississippi to visit my grandmother. Do you remember her? No, what am I thinking? Of course, she died before you were born, but you know where I mean, Mother's place, Granddaddy's farm."

"Sue, just go on with the story." Nancy's father looked up from his plate and the rose catalog opened next to it. "I've never known anybody get balled up in details the way you do."

"Well, I used to play with a black girl. I can't even remember her name, but she was a girl who lived on the place. I liked her very much, and once I asked Grandma if she could spend the night. Grandma said yes, but we had to sleep on the porch. It was summertime. I didn't think much about it, but after the girl left, my grandmother burned the nightgown we'd lent her to wear that night."

Nancy and her father both sat back in their chairs and stared at Mrs. Martin.

"Mother! How horrible!"

"Yes, it was, wasn't it?" Her mother sounded like she was talking in her sleep.

"You know, Sue, these Delta Gothic tales of yours are sometimes rather hard to believe."

"I don't know what your life was like up in Chicago, dear, but down here that's just the way it was." Mrs. Martin stared out the window with an odd expression. "I didn't think things had really changed, could change, until today, when I saw that girl in Nancy's room."

"So what are you saying, Mother?"

"Just be careful." Her mother seemed to snap back to the dinner table. "Be careful. Friendships between people of very different backgrounds just don't work. I know. You could be setting yourself up for a lot of heartbreak."

CHAPTER 8

▼

GIVE HIM THE BALL

From the Forrest bench, Eddie watched Pineville's two black players huddle with the white players. All of them came out slapping their hands together. The black boys both lined up on play after play, catching passes, taking hand-offs, marching up and down the field as if they owned it. The Pineville crowd cheered whether a black player had the ball or a white one. Why shouldn't they? They were whipping up on Forrest, a team they hadn't beaten in eight years. The score was 14-3, and it was just the first quarter. Coach Ezell was fuming.

"Your boys sure aren't doing much," a voice behind Eddie said.

Eddie spun around and grinned. Coach Frazier and Vernell leaned against the fence. Over the sound of the band and the chanting of the cheerleaders, Eddie leaned over the fence.

"Hey, Coach! What you doing here?"

"We don't play tonight, Eddie, so Vernell and I thought we'd run out and see how old Steady Eddie, the preacher's boy, is doing."

Eddie's face hardened. They looked at each other.

"Humm, I see," said Coach Frazier.

"I thought they were going to play you tonight, Eddie," Vernell said quietly. "Man, that's ridiculous. It's the next-to-the-last game!"

Coach Frazier placed his finger over his lips and pointed at Coach Ezell. "I said your boys aren't doing much of nothing," he repeated, louder.

Coach Ezell slowly turned around, glaring, his jaw muscles working. When he saw Coach Frazier, he slumped. "Oh, hell," he muttered and turned back to the field.

Coach Frazier grinned and chuckled, a dry, "Heh, heh, heh."

Another cheer burst from the Pineville side of the field.

"Sorry I made you miss that play, Ezell. They made a first down."

Joe Jackson, a black player, broke through the Forrest line and sprinted for twelve yards before Art Gaston, a Forrest defensive back, tripped him up.

"Yeah, sure can't win playing colored boys, can you?" Coach Frazier said loudly.

Coach Ezell threw down his playbook.

"Time out on the field," said the mellow voice over the PA system. The bands struck up rival fight songs.

Coach Frazier folded his big arms on top of the fence and looked out over the field. Eddie turned and leaned back, his shoulder just touching his former coach's arm. Vernell put a foot up on the chain link and watched the play.

Forrest stopped a running play up the middle. Pineville was going to have to kick. Eddie could hear the cheerleaders chanting, vaguely aware of the dazzle of blue and gold every time he looked at Coach Frazier. *Don't so much as look at a white girl,* he thought.

"Looks like Pineville's got itself a *team,*" Coach Frazier bellowed. Coach Ezell's shoulders twitched.

"I were you, Ezell, I'd be sick of letting myself lose just because you got this idea on you about Negroes," Coach Frazier said. This time, Coach Ezell did not turn or twitch.

Coach Frazier winked at Eddie and Vernell. Vernell laughed, but Eddie just shook his head.

After the kick, Coach Ezell looked at Eddie, then at Coach Frazier. The Forrest offensive players bounced on the balls of their feet, impatient to get back on the field, waiting for Coach to call their numbers, slap them on the shoulder, send them out. Instead, Coach looked hard at Eddie. Coach Frazier smiled a crooked grin.

"Russell, out on the field. You're at fullback. C-22-right."

Eddie felt like his body was slowly filling with ice water. It gripped his legs, then his heart, his throat, his head. He took a step and then another, discovering that he could move even though he was frozen. His body took over, while his mind floated somewhere above, watching with icy calm.

The boys ran onto the field, clapping their hands, not looking at Eddie, but he saw a couple of them exchanging sly grins. The center, a quiet boy named Dougie Hermidinger, bent over and gripped the ball. Spencer lined up to the left of center. In C-22-right, the fullback, Eddie this time, was supposed to run to the right of center after a simple handoff from the quarterback. Townsend's white teeth gleamed behind the single bar of his helmet. Eddie had a bad feeling.

The line went down in their three-point stances, knuckles digging into the cold grass. Hermidinger snapped the ball, Townsend took it and spun halfway around. He thrust the ball at Eddie, pulled it quickly back, then pushed it out again. The fake made Eddie miss the handoff. He overshot Townsend, and grabbed back desperately at the football on the second thrust. He had it for a moment and then felt it slip through his hands like a greased watermelon.

The football bounced around like a mad thing. Everyone jumped at it, tried to fall on it, tried to pick it up, tried to find it. Finally it came squirting out of a Pineville player's hands. Eddie made a blind grab, felt the ball, grabbed it, tucked it into his belly, and fell down. He felt other bodies falling on his, digging at the ball, trying to dislodge it. Eddie held on, eyes closed, curled in fetal position around the hard lump of leather.

"A fumble on the play. Forrest recovers," the announcer said. "Second and eight. Time out Forrest."

Around Eddie players got to their feet, helping each other up. No one reached out a hand to him. He got up, tossed the ball to the ref and trotted off the field, the last of the players to get to the sideline. A couple of the players punched each other, snickering, and he heard Townsend's loud, high laugh.

The laughter stopped when the players got to the sideline and saw their coach's eyes. He looked like an atomic bomb about to detonate. Coach Frazier watched from the other side of the fence, his eyes hard. Eddie stopped a few steps short of the huddle around Coach Ezell.

"Townsend, take off your helmet."

The players all gasped. Taking off your helmet meant you weren't going to play. You were benched.

"Coach!" Townsend protested. "I didn't do nothing. The nigger fumbled, is all."

Coach Ezell leaped at Townsend, who backed up two quick steps. "*You* fumbled," Ezell said. "Russell recovered. He wants to win; apparently you don't. Now take off your helmet and sit down. I don't want your butt to come off that bench for the rest of this game. You stand up, you're going to the bus. Is that clear to you?"

The last remnants of smirk left Townsend's face. He cast a poisonous look at Eddie, snatched his helmet off and threw himself down on the bench. He flung his helmet so hard on the ground it bounced up and hit Spencer in the kneecap. Spencer bit his lip and shook his leg.

"Fletcher?" Coach Ezell shouted.

"Yes, sir," said a thin, scared voice. Marvin Fletcher, the sophomore backup quarterback, had never played a down because Touchdown Townsend never got sick or hurt or tired.

"You're it. Let's go. Everybody back out. C-22-left."

"Left," piped Fletcher. They clapped their hands in a disorganized syncopation and trotted out onto the field.

This time Eddie watched carefully, sure Fletcher wouldn't try the same trick, but Eddie knew Fletcher might botch the handoff anyway, from sheer terror. A nervous shiver went down the line as the unfamiliar voice quavered out the numbers. Fletcher's "Hike!" came out in a shriek, but they all somehow leapt forward together. Eddie felt like he was running toward Fletcher in slow motion. The terrified sophomore held the ball out, his hands visibly trembling. Eddie took the ball firmly, tucked it away, and then he was back in real time.

He exploded forward, saw Spencer clear a space to the left of center. He shot through, hands desperately grabbing at him. He gunned forward and then felt arms wrapping around his legs from behind. Eyes fixed on the white yard marker ahead of him, he dragged his opponent forward three more steps and then fell with a grunt, clutching the ball, his heart racing. Oh, God, it felt good.

"First down," he heard over the PA.

*   *   *   *

"Lakeesha! Eddie was great!" Nancy had spotted Lakeesha as they were leaving and pushed her way to her. The crowd jostled them against each other as the fans surged through the gates and into the black night. The game had ended in a 17-17 tie, which was frustrating, but somehow Nancy felt more optimistic than she had all season.

"Yes, but we didn't *win!*" Lakeesha said, almost in tears.

"But we tied, and that's better than losing week after week, like we've been doing." Nancy paused and glanced at Lakeesha's parents, who had stopped and were politely waiting for the girls to finish their conversation.

Lakeesha looked flustered.

"Mama, Daddy, this is Nancy Martin."

They all shook hands. Nancy stared at Lakeesha's father's collar. "Are you a minister?" she asked.

"Yes, indeed I am." His smile didn't reach his eyes. "You must visit our church sometime."

"I will," she said. Then she felt shivery. Would she go to a black church? Nancy opened her mouth to say she had forgotten, she had to do something in her own church on Sunday. The next second, she was furious with herself. Of course she would. "Really," she said, with a bright smile. "I will."

Reverend Russell's smile vanished. "Ten o'clock Sunday," he said. "If you come, you must stay and have Sunday dinner. We always have a community lunch after church."

"I will. I'll come."

They said polite good-byes, and Nancy walked away through the shoving crowd, thinking that maybe all the adventure in life wasn't in Paris.

CHAPTER 9

▼

A SANCTIFIED WITNESS

Nancy drove her mother's car across the railroad track a quarter mile down the road from her house and onto the soft yellow dirt, winding among hummocks covered with kudzu vine.

She'd had a bit of a battle, first to get permission to go to the black church, and second to use the car. Her Dad never let anyone else drive his car. She had prevailed in large part because her mother had a migraine, and her parents had decided not to go to church that morning.

Now she was late. She accelerated, and the car skidded. She slowed down, heart racing.

When she got to Hattie's house, she could see the neat red brick church on the highway, its parking lot filled with cars. She pulled in with a crunch of gravel, slammed the car door and hurried toward the church door, high heels wobbling. The sound of singing coming through the windows made her heart race with the realization of how late she was. Nancy ran up the steps and opened the door, surprised to find herself right inside the church. Everyone was just sitting down. She slipped into a seat on the aisle in the very back row.

The music stopped, and an older man in a tan suit read from the Bible in a rhythmical voice. Sweat dripped down Nancy's back although the day was cool and clear. She looked straight ahead, but she felt dark eyes flickering toward her and away. She took a deep breath, trying to make it soundless.

As the man in the tan suit sat down, Nancy looked cautiously around her. The church had plain white walls and clear glass windows, each with one pane of brightly colored glass in the middle, green, blue, red. A woman in a dark green choir robe with gold collar and sleeve linings began to sing.

Nancy realized that she was afraid, really afraid. Her knees quivered, and her hands shook. She wiped her palms on her green tweed skirt, pulling the hem down over her knees. She tried to lean back and listen to the woman's powerful voice, but instead she looked sideways at the people in her pew. A little boy in a dark suit and tie wiggled and stared at her. His mother grabbed his arm and yanked, looking at Nancy out of the corners of her eyes.

By leaning sideways a fraction of an inch, she saw Lakeesha and Eddie on the front row. Eddie slowly turned his head around as if he felt her gaze and looked right at her. Nancy tried to smile at him, but her lips quivered. Eddie held her gaze for a long moment and then nodded, turning quickly back around.

A girl about her own age two rows ahead turned and looked around, saw Nancy and frowned. *She must have seen Eddie looking at me*, Nancy thought.

Nancy looked around. Everyone seemed happy, in their Sunday best. A little girl in a heavily ruffled white dress jumped up and down on the faded red carpet of the aisle. Nancy thought of all the times her mother had shushed and frowned at her when she wiggled in church.

Gradually she realized that Reverend Russell had begun his sermon.

He looked out over the congregation, his voice calm and thought-ful. "We are the children of Cain. We all bear the mark of murder and violence upon our hearts. That is our heritage. Cain slew his brother Abel. He struck and killed him in a rage. What sparked that first murder? Did Abel taunt his brother? Ridicule him?

"We are the children of Cain," he repeated. "Our violent natures urge us to meet insults with threats and violence with greater violence. But if we are to return to our God, the Lord of all, we must rise above our heritage of hate. And we *shall* rise above hate and murder."

Reverend Russell struck the pulpit hard. His voice rose, he spread his arms out to either side, stiff as the wings of a Dutch windmill.

"The world will bear witness to our struggle if we ourselves bear no stain of hate and violence." Reverend Russell lowered his arms and his voice, gripped the lectern and leaned toward his congregation. "We can transform the world. No power is stronger than the power of a righteous idea."

"Yes, Lord!" shouted the man next to Nancy. She jumped.

"No strength is greater than the strength of innocence!"

"Amen!" called a woman close to the front.

"We shall bow our heads to those who hate us."

"Oh, tell it!"

"We shall turn the other cheek to those who strike us."

"We will!"

"We shall confront our enemies."

"Sweet Jesus!"

"We shall look into the eyes of our enemies and find in them something to love."

Reverend Russell looked across the church at Nancy. Her face was red and hot.

"You know it, brother!" someone shouted.

"Not one of us is too weak or afraid to witness the struggle." He kept his eyes locked on hers, until she looked down at her hands, clenched on the hem on her green velvet jacket.

"Not one! Not one."

"If we do this, we *shall* overcome. We *shall* overcome. We *shall* overcome."

The whole congregation leaped up, chanting with him. Nancy rose, her knees still shaky. She couldn't chant, but tears sprang to her eyes when the choir began singing, an unfamiliar hymn, full of joy and triumph.

Their beautiful voices shook the church. Everyone clapped and sang and swayed. Nancy clapped her hands softly, unable to sing. Was she the enemy? Did all these people hate her? The little girl in white lace spun around in the aisle, clapping.

Reverend Russell stood in the pulpit, unsmiling, his hands clasped in front of him, resting on the Bible. He looked at Nancy, and he nodded his head once.

Nancy could see the back of Eddie's head and thought suddenly that maybe Reverend Russell should have preached a sermon on Abraham and Isaac rather than Cain and Abel.

After church, Eddie and Lakeesha took Nancy through the line to get their plates of fried chicken and cornbread, greens and peas from the church supper tables. They carried them to the back of Uncle Rayburn's pick-up truck. In the bright October sun, a tree tossed in the wind over their heads, sending circles of light and shade dancing over their faces. Across the parking lot, at a series of wooden tables, other members of the congregation were eating, talking, laughing.

As they ate, Eddie stiffened every time Nancy spoke. He found himself unable to meet her eyes again but watched her sideways, following her gaze. He saw her look over at Rochelle sitting with Clifford. A curdled red stained her cheeks and neck, and she ran her hand along the back of her neck, lifting the silky red hair into the stiff October breeze.

Eddie felt something uncoil inside him, the iron control relaxing for a moment in the safety of the churchyard, among his own family and people. He looked straight at her.

She smiled at him. "It must be great, Eddie, to be playing again." Nancy bit her lip and blushed even redder.

Eddie paused a minute before answering. He groped for words to describe that sense of abandonment to the moment, the hurling of his body, sure and swift, toward the ball and then down the field.

"Yeah, it's great. I just go where the ball is." He felt the truth of it and smiled.

Just then they heard the snarl of an unmuffled car engine. A Chevy topped the hill and roared down toward them. A distorted white face leaned out the window, screaming something that couldn't quite be heard over the engine. A bottle flew from the car as it passed, breaking on the road and in the gravel churchyard. Brown glass sprayed up around them with the sour smell of beer.

The girls screamed and ducked behind Eddie. Eddie's smile vanished. He stared without expression at the cloud of exhaust that blew across the road. In the distance, invisible now, the growling engine changed gears, shifting down, began to grow fainter. People rushed from the picnic tables over to them.

"White trash!" Rochelle's clear voice shattered the shocked silence.

Rochelle's mother jerked at her arm. "You hush, girl!"

Hattie pushed her way through to put one arm around Nancy and the other around Lakeesha. Eddie saw his mother at the edge of the crowd, her hands clutched together.

Reverend Russell clasped his hands and said, "Let us pray."

Eddie didn't hear a word of his father's prayer. Instead, over and over, he heard the words, *"You cannot so much as look a white girl in the face. That will get you hurt faster than anything else."*

"Amen," Eddie said, when his father's prayer ended.

CHAPTER 10

▼

THE SMOKING CLUB

The next day, Eddie passed the smoking club on his way to shop class, giving it a wide berth, as usual. He noticed Townsend hanging out there, laughing it up. Coach would be on his ass if he caught him smoking, Eddie thought.

He walked into the classroom just behind Spencer. His eyes went immediately to his bookcase. Neatly shellacked to the side was a yellow leaflet that read, "BE A MAN. JOIN THE KLAN."

It was the latest assault on his bookcase. Every day when he came into shop, something had happened to it—a dent, as if someone had dropped a hammer on it, or a splatter of white paint.

Once overnight one of his long side pieces had been neatly cut in two. Mr. Young had taken the piece and cut it into smaller pieces and made everyone in class practice dovetailing over and over until the pieces were so tiny you could barely get them into the miter boxes. Len had loudly blamed the extra work on "the nigger" when Mr. Young left the room.

Coach Frazier had been right. "Boy" would have sounded like a compliment now.

Dozier laughed at Eddie's expression and swaggered across the room in front of them. Spencer stuck his foot out. Len fell hard, stretching his full length on the floor. He leaped to his feet, blood spurting from his nose, his fist clenched. "You dare trip a white man?" he shouted at Eddie.

"He didn't trip you, Dozier. I did," Spencer said.

Mr. Young came into the room. He looked from the boys, to Eddie's bookcase, and then back to Len Dozier. Then he went to the shelves behind his desk and handed Eddie a sanding block.

"It should be easy to remove the offensive material, Mr. Russell. This will certainly be a piece with a history."

He looked at Len. "Mr. Dozier, you may be excused to clean the gore from your ignoble visage."

✳   ✳   ✳   ✳

Eddie got to the gym early that day after school and opened his locker. It was empty. *So*, he thought, *they've kicked me off the team.* He slammed his hand into the locker door and then shook the whole section of lockers, banging his door over and over. He kicked the flimsy gray metal, and the section rocked backward. Eddie looked around through a haze of fury and saw Fletcher's pale face peeking around the corner.

"Eddie? You all right?" Fletcher sounded like a little bird chirping.

"No, I am *not* all right, man. They've taken my stuff. I'm off the team."

"No, they didn't. Coach just moved it. I saw him. Your locker's over here now."

Rubbing his knuckles, Eddie followed Fletcher around the corner. Fletcher pointed at a locker right in the middle of the line that was the exclusive turf of the first-string players. Eddie opened it. It was his, all right.

"What are you doing here?" Townsend's voice drawled behind him. "Your locker's back there."

"Damned if I know," Eddie muttered.

A whistle blew sharply behind them, making them all jump. Coach stood there, hands on hips.

"I'm making a few changes this week, boys. This is one of them. Hop to it. We've got a long practice."

They suited up, Eddie and Townsend pulling on their pads and jerseys trying not to look at each other or touch each other. The team trudged out to the field. As usual, Eddie trailed a few feet behind and lined up for jumping jacks in his regular place, a little to the side with a good big space around him. He'd been in that position ever since the practice when Townsend had asked to move.

Coach Ezell stood at the front of the group, running his hand over his freshly trimmed black crew cut. They waited for him to bark out the command to start jumping. Instead he glared at them in silence. They glanced at each other, rolling shoulders, shifting feet.

"Russell!" Coach shouted.

"Sir!" Eddie shouted back.

"Up here, front and center."

Eddie froze for a second and then walked forward and took a place at the center of the front row. Dougie and Fletcher moved aside to make room for him.

"Okay, team! Jumping jacks until I say stop."

Another ripple flashed across the field. Usually they did 50 jumping jacks, not in unison, some fast, some slow. Whenever a boy hit 50, he'd stop and rest, waiting until the last one finished, usually either Spencer or Dougie.

That was just the beginning. They did jumping jacks, push-ups, knee bends, and running in place in unison for half an hour. Then they drilled under the lights until nearly nine o'clock. A cold front blew through, and the boys shivered in the icy wind.

For the first time, Eddie practiced with the first string. He took handoff after handoff from Touchdown Townsend. He caught passes from Townsend. He blocked for Townsend when they practiced bootlegs or quarterback sneaks.

"Don't block the heart, Russell," Coach yelled at him once when he blocked Bobby Davidson, who slipped right past. "You know these boys don't have hearts. Block across the whole body; that way he can't get around you."

When Coach finally called it quits, the team left the field groaning. Eddie stood waiting for Coach to yell, "Okay, Russell, extra laps." Instead, Coach looked at him and said, "Okay, Russell, hit the showers." Eddie's heart leaped at finally not having to run extra laps and then sank when he thought of the showers. He followed the line of tired players off the field, down the road to the gym, into the locker room, Coach Ezell right behind him.

Half the players were already naked under the steaming set of showerheads, scrubbing, groaning, laughing, wet and pink. He'd never seen them undressed. He stopped and got a sharp poke in the back from Coach Ezell's index finger. Eddie forced himself to move down the aisle to his new locker. Spencer, his big belly quivering over a white towel wrapped around his waist, stepped aside for him to pass without looking up. Eddie prayed that everyone else would also ignore him.

He glanced behind him. Coach pointed at the shower. The babble of voices ebbed as the boys realized what was happening. They hurried to change as Eddie slowly stripped off his shoes, his socks, his soaked jersey and pants, his pads. He stopped and looked behind him again. Coach stood there still, like a statue, nodding once at Eddie, his whistle clenched between his teeth.

Grabbing a towel in one hand, Eddie quickly stripped off his underwear and whipped the towel around his waist, his private parts shriveling and his heart pounding.

At his first step forward, the white boys began to bolt out of the showers. Coach blew the whistle, ringing like a siren in their ears. "You will stay in the showers until I tell you to come out. Fletcher, you can get dressed. Smith, Russell, get in there. You've had a long, cold practice. Now you need a long, hot shower."

With one quick glance at each other, Spencer and Eddie walked into the steaming spray of hot water, flicking their towels over the bar outside the showers. Eddie turned to face the wall, closed his eyes and let the water flow over him, drowning all sound, all sights. He tried to drift away from the locker room, float in some gray limbo. But someone prodded his shoulder, hard. He opened his eyes, and turned his head. Coach Ezell stood there, a tight grin on his face, holding out a bar of soap. Eddie took it and lathered up, realizing to his horror that Townsend was right beside him.

Gradually, the voices started up again, Coach started letting the other boys out of the showers. But he kept Spencer, Townsend and Eddie under the showers what seemed like hours and made them get out at the same time. They had to dress together, close together. Their elbows touched. Drops of water flew through the air from one to the other.

When Coach Ezell finally walked away, Spencer laughed and slammed his locker door. "So Coach finally wants us to be a team again. About time."

Eddie thought it might be more that he wanted to avoid a lawsuit.

Townsend turned and glared at Eddie without speaking. Eddie stuck his head into his locker, wanting to just crawl in and close the door behind him.

That night was just the beginning. All week, old drills, new drills. Weird things like climbing up on the goal posts and dropping down into the arms of their teammates. On Tuesday, Townsend ran five extra laps when he let Eddie hit the ground.

Over and over they huddled and slapped hands and shouted "TEAM" at the top of their lungs.

They left the gym late every night, with their bags in their hands, and stepped into their parents' waiting cars, breath steaming. Once Eddie heard Townsend say, before his car door slammed, "That nigger! This is all his fault."

CHAPTER 11

▼

JUST LOOK AT HIM GO

On Friday night, a damp wind blew over the Forrest football field. Nancy gave her blue-and-gold pom-poms a shake. The stands were about three-quarters full of gloomy fans. Only three minutes left in the last game of the year, and the score had been stuck at 10-7 the wrong way since midway through the first quarter.

This week the ribbons everyone wore said, "Whip West Side," their greatest traditional rival, a big, rough, county high school, still all-white.

West Side did not have a particularly good team this year, but they had managed to hang in against the much more talented Forrest squad. The close score had aroused some excitement for a while, but now everybody was beginning to believe that 10-7 would be it. Some fans had already given up and were beginning to trudge out of the stadium.

Nancy saw the Russells two rows up in the stands. She realized that the space that everyone had carefully left around them earlier in the season had slowly over the season shrunk to almost nothing.

She looked out over the heads of the football players to the field. Eddie had been in nearly the whole game. Even from where Nancy stood, she could see the punishment he was taking, the ruthless late hits, the deliberate kicks when the refs' backs were turned. Sometimes the refs' backs were turned on purpose, or they were oddly struck blind. Missy started a cheer. They jumped and shouted, but the crowd barely reacted. Shaking her head, Missy turned back to the field.

"We're only three points behind, close enough to kick a field goal. Doesn't anyone care? I guess we're just jinxed." She clapped twice, significantly. The other girls nodded, their faces hard.

Nancy narrowed her blue eyes and stared at Missy, who shrugged and turned her back, tossing her frizzing curls.

✳   ✳   ✳   ✳

Out on the field, the low chant started again, "nigger-lover, nig-ger-lover, nigger-lover," right down the West Side defensive line. The Forrest offense kept their heads down, but Eddie could see their hands and shoulders twitch.

That was nothing compared to what Eddie was hearing at the bottom of a pile of white boys. "We'll cut your balls off, boy," "Go back to your mama, boy," and over and over again, "Nigger, nigger, nig-ger."

He shut the taunts out of his mind, got into position behind Townsend, who leaned over with his hands between the center's legs, waiting for the ball. Eddie checked his blockers and went down into his three-point stance, as he had over and over all night. The wet November game seemed to have lasted since the beginning of time. It was second down and a long six yards to go for Forrest.

Eddie looked over Spencer's shoulder at Buster Bostick, a West Side defensive linesman with a big red face and sneering blue eyes, about all he could see through the helmet.

Eddie lined up behind and to the left of Townsend, directly behind Spencer.

Nose to nose with Spencer, Buster spoke in a loud, raspy voice. "Hey, you take showers with that nigger?"

Eddie suddenly understood how much these boys hated him because he hated them back. He shook, not with fear, but rage. He wanted revenge. He wanted to kill.

Spencer gave one sharp grunt and came off the line like a Clydesdale stallion. In one fluid motion, he brought his crossed arms up under Buster's chin and tossed him on his butt like a rag doll.

Spencer glared down at his victim. "Take that, Nazi!"

Whistles blew hysterically.

"A flag on the play," the announcer said.

Forrest's fans groaned as the ref chopped the side of his hand against his arm and backed the team up not just five yards for being offsides but a full fifteen yards for a personal foul, unsportsmanlike behavior. Second down and 21 yards to go. Not only that, the penalty had pushed them back out of the range of their field goal kicker.

But when Eddie glanced around, he saw the other players grinning. Dougie slapped Spencer on the back. That was weird. They should all be upset, but instead they seemed elated.

Jerry Woodward, a second-string tight end, ran into the huddle. "T-18-left," he said.

T-18-left was nothing terribly imaginative—Touchdown Townsend was supposed to drop back and pass to the end, in this case Jerry. The offensive line would surge to the left, and Eddie had to come across the line and pick up the block on Bostick. He couldn't believe he was getting a chance to lay a hit on the bastard.

They all clapped their hands and went into position. A galvanizing energy cracked down the offensive line. Eddie shuddered, feeling it wash over him. He looked over to the sidelines. Coach Ezell's fanatic blue-white eyes glinted as he smacked his rolled-up playbook against the palm of his hand.

The ball was snapped, and the offensive line surged forward in front of Eddie. "What's gotten into them?" he thought. "They're not that good!"

Eddie swept forward, took a bead on Bostick, and charged forward as hard as he could. Forget the heart, forget the body. Eddie threw his whole body in a killer block right at Bostick's knees. He wasn't trying to knock Bostick down; he was trying to break his legs. Bostick went down screaming.

Eddie's hate evaporated in the instant of contact. That hadn't been an adrenaline-rushed hard block. It had been a personal assault. Eddie knew the difference. His head felt like it was full of helium and lights danced at the edges of his vision. *Please don't let me throw up,* he prayed.

A few feet to Eddie's left, Jerry Woodward slipped on the wet grass. Left holding the ball, Townsend looked desperately left and right. When he saw the hole Eddie had opened, he darted through and gained three yards.

Buster struggled to his feet, a trickle of blood dripping from his nose. He narrowed his bitter blue eyes at Eddie and said clearly and loudly, "You should be picking cotton, nigger. Not playing football with white men."

Townsend got up and looked at Bostick, then at Eddie and then at Spencer. Eddie couldn't read Townsend's expression through the bars of his helmet.

Eddie walked slowly back to his place, his head clearing with each step. With the clock rolling inexorably down, they were going without a huddle. Spencer was down already in his three-point stance. As Eddie passed, Spencer winked.

As soon as Bostick was across from him, before Townsend even started the count, Spencer shot up and tossed Buster on his back for the third time.

On the next play, third and 33 after Spencer's second personal foul, Forrest made only five yards on Eddie's run up the middle. They were on their own 45-yard line, 55 yards from the goal line.

They punted to West Side, whose deep man caught the ball in the end zone and tried to run it out instead of just going down on one knee, which would have let them start at the 20-yard-line.

"What an idiot!" Spencer muttered to Eddie.

*   *   *   *

Even from the track, Nancy caught the difference in the attitude of the Forrest boys toward Eddie as Buster was helped from the field by two of his teammates. They allowed themselves to touch Eddie, casually bumping him in the huddle.

Forrest tackled the runner on the five-yard line. When play started again, Forrest's defense was so fired up that in three plays, West Side went only three yards.

The West Side punter stood in the end zone and shook his hands nervously, waiting for the snap. The fans were now going crazy. Nancy couldn't even hear the other cheerleaders over the roaring and stamping. "Block that kick! Block that kick! Forrest, Forrest, Forrest!" Then everyone roared like lions, making the stands shake. Nancy felt the rumble through the soles of her feet and in her collarbones.

She stood on tiptoe to see Eddie's parents. They were standing, like everyone else, but did not join the cheers. They never had. Eddie's mother had her hand on the sleeve of her husband's black coat.

Nancy whirled back around just in time to see the West Side center snap the ball, too high. The scrawny bare-footed West Side punter jumped to get it. He barely got the kick off when a flying body came across the line of the ball's trajectory and made a solid thumping block.

The stands erupted in pandemonium. On the field, the players rolled in a confused jumble. Eddie Russell had blocked the punt. Spencer Smith had downed it on the two-yard line.

The cheerleaders leaped into the air. Their pom-poms shook in blue-and-gold frenzy. The players on the sidelines jumped up and down, up and down. The band's trumpets blared. The drums beat wildly. The tuba throbbed.

Coach Ezell threw down his rolled-up playbook and thrust one arm after the other into the air. Nancy drew in a long breath that was almost a sob and looked around and up to find Eddie's people. In the stands, fans pounded Reverend and Mrs. Russell on their backs and pumped their hands in ecstasy. Nancy couldn't see Lakeesha, but she saw Rochelle at the very top of the stands, waving her arms around over her head.

⁎   ⁎   ⁎   ⁎

Eight seconds were left in the game. The ref carefully placed the ball on the two-yard line. Coach gathered his electrified players around him, his eyes blazing. "C-22-left," he said.

Eddie looked at Townsend, remembering the last time they had played C-22-left, but he couldn't see Townsend's eyes. The players all nodded. The second-string players came forward; the whole squad locked hands, and shouted "TEAM!" Fletcher's voice quavered above them all.

When Dougie snapped the ball, Townsend handed it off to Eddie, clean and solid. Spencer fell forward like a grain silo, crushing the defensive line. A huge hole opened. Eddie tucked the ball hard under his right arm, tight against his stomach. He charged across the goal line, untouched, bodies rolling to his right and left. Under the goal posts, he raised the ball over his head and turned around. His teammates charged him, jumping and screaming.

The band struck up the battle hymn; the cheerleaders sang and danced.

Oh they call him Mr. Touchdown,
Oh, yes they call him Mr. T.
He can run and he can throw,

Give him the ball and just
Look at him go.

Eddie stood in the end zone, the ball high in one hand, exalted, although his face was as impassive as ever. The faces of his teammates seemed supernaturally clear. He looked back to the stands, toward his parents, but saw only a confused blur of motion and color. The team swarmed around him; they pummeled his arms and back. Spencer hugged him, lifting him off his feet and into the air. Only Touchdown Townsend stood still and silent at the edge of the end zone. Eddie knew this should have been Townsend's moment, the winning play of his last high school game. Townsend should have been the one carried off the field on his teammates' shoulders.

But the band played, and the fans sang Mr. Touchdown, for him, Eddie Russell. If he had made a million touchdowns, blocked a billion punts at Douglass, it would never have been like this. His rage and fear vanished in the ecstasy of victory. The tight control he had locked onto his soul since the day the men from the NAACP came to his home wavered. Then it broke.

Eddie leaped into the air with the white boys, shouting.

CHAPTER 12

▼

THE CARPET TOO
IS MOVING
UNDER YOU

In the girls' bathroom under the stands, Nancy locked herself into a stall and leaned her head against the door. All the cheerleaders were in the bathroom, yelling and doing their hair and makeup, but Nancy needed a moment alone, to savor certain things about the night that the others couldn't understand, the triumph she felt for Eddie and Lakeesha. For their parents. She was almost angry with the other cheerleaders. Now they were talking about Eddie like he was a big hero, which he was, and like they had never called him a jinx and refused to talk to his sister. How could they just switch so fast, not admit anything, not apologize? Then Nancy laughed. *Not tell me I was right*, she thought.

Then she heard boys' voices from the other side of the thin wall, where the boys' bathroom was.

"That jig's going to be even more uppity after this."

"Damn right."

"We're going to have to do something."

"Cain't just sit back and take it."

"Damn right."

A toilet flushing drowned the voices. Nancy stood frozen. She should go out and tell someone, but who? She had to get out of there and go with her friends to the Pig and Whistle for barbecue, but she was afraid. Most of all, she was afraid that one of those voices was Larry "Touchdown" Townsend's.

*   *   *   *

Eddie slowed down when he saw his father standing by the door of the car. His stomach knotted. Then he picked up his pace again, anxious to get it over with.

"Quite a hero, aren't you, son?" His father spoke so quietly no one in the car could have heard him.

Eddie squinted to see inside the car, relieved it was only his mother and Mouse inside. Rochelle and Etta Lee must have gone home with Clifford.

"No, sir."

"Yes, you are and you know you are. I am proud of you, son. You've stuck it out and made your mark."

His father stopped speaking and the silence stretched out between them until Eddie couldn't stand it anymore and spoke. "I lost control tonight, Dad. I wanted to kill that boy, that Bostick boy. I hit him too hard. It was a clip. I should have gotten a penalty. I—"

"I know. I saw it," his father said. "You acted on what you felt. You cannot do that, Eddie. You cannot! You cannot let violence gain the upper hand."

Eddie looked at the ground, his jaw clenched, teeth grinding. "No, sir, I won't."

"Eddie, no one else will remember what you did. No one else even noticed. It's been wiped out by your blocking that punt and making that touchdown. Things are going to be very different for you from now on. But you and I, we know. Be careful, son. Be careful."

His father reached out then and gave him a brief hug. Eddie swallowed around the knot in his throat. The hug seemed to be a signal and his mother and Lakeesha jumped out of the car and began hugging him too, congratulating him, and crying.

Women are lucky, he thought. *It's okay if they cry.*

*   *   *   *

The last day of school before the Christmas holidays dawned cold and dark. Eddie blew his breath out in a long plume of white mist as he walked across the parking lot toward the shop building. It was early, classes wouldn't start for another half-hour, but Eddie was worried about his bookcase. He'd finally finished it the night before, put on the last coat of varnish. He hadn't been able to sleep the night before, worrying that somehow, something else was going to happen to it. He ran into the shop building and up the worn wooden stairs, rubbing his cold hands together.

He stopped as if he'd hit an electric fence. Len Dozier stood alone in the middle of the shop. Eddie's bookcase had been yanked to the middle of the room. Len raised a heavy metal mallet and brought it down with a crash. The wood cracked with a sound like a gunshot, and the mallet bounced back, twisting Len's skinny wrist.

Wincing, Len shook his hand. "Damned nigger!" he muttered and raised the mallet again, but a meaty hand grabbed his wrist. Eddie had been so focused on Len he hadn't seen Mr. Young come into the room from the other door.

Len twisted and tried to swing the mallet. Mr. Young's hand squeezed hard. Len yelped with pain and dropped the mallet on his foot, yelping again.

"It does not surprise me, Mr. Dozier, that you are so unfamiliar with my habits as to think you could get to my shop before I arrive in the morning," Mr. Young said. "It is my habit to rise early and break my fast in my shop shortly after dawn. That is fortunate, I believe. For Mr. Russell, that is, not for you, sir." Mr. Young nodded at Eddie, who stood frozen in the doorway.

Len felt the movement of Mr. Young's head and twisted around to see Eddie standing in the door. "Oh, shit! That god-damned nigger is everywhere!"

"Mr. Dozier, at last I believe this wanton vandalism will be sufficient to have you removed permanently from these hallowed halls."

Len twisted again. "Oh, cut the bullshit, you old queer," he hissed.

Eddie stepped aside as Mr. Young wrestled Dozier out the door and down the stairs. He looked at his broken, twisted bookcase. Pain kicked him in the stomach. He spun around and ran back out the door and down the stairs.

All around him, kids bubbled with holiday spirits, scuffled good-naturedly, laughed. Only a half-day of school and then home for the Christmas holidays.

He almost knocked Rochelle down as he barreled along not looking where he was going. She grabbed his arm. "Did you hear?" she asked.

"Hear what?"

"Lethe made the highest score in the school on the National Achievement Tests!"

"Whoa!" he said, but his heart wasn't in it.

"Yes! She got so quiet when she heard I thought she was going to bust."

"Who told her?"

"That bitch Granger!"

"Rochelle, come on." Eddie glanced around.

"Well, all right, it's Christmas so I'll just call her an old bag. How's that?"

Eddie rolled his eyes, and they walked on toward the shop building, Rochelle talking away about Lethe, about the holidays, not noticing Eddie's silence.

Rochelle cut away at the door to her home ec class, and Eddie's feet dragged him up the stairs to the shop room. He leaned against the door, looking in again at the mangled bookcase lying now on a table in the middle of the room.

Dead silence filled the room, broken only by a few nervous whispers and rustles as one by one the boys came into the shop class.

"Mr. Russell!" boomed Mr. Young, coming down the hall and stopping at the door. "Mr. Russell, sir, I cannot walk through you."

Eddie stepped numbly aside for Mr. Young to enter the room, and then turned away so the other boys couldn't see his face.

"Why so silent and glum, boys? Your projects are finished. We had planned to merely occupy space today. It appears to me that we now have more meaningful work at hand. Mr. Russell has placed a challenge before us. Can we, class, rectify the seemingly hopeless disaster we see before us? I think so! We have but to begin."

The boys just stared at Mr. Young, wrinkling their noses and foreheads.

"What's the old windbag talking about?" Eddie heard back-up quarterback Marvin Fletcher whisper to Spencer.

Mr. Young gestured toward the bashed bookcase. "Mr. Smith. What do you see before you?"

"It's busted, sir," Spencer said.

"Mr. Smith, you will have to be more specific, if not more grammatical. What exactly is the condition of this piece? Tell me precisely, if you please."

"Well, its top shelf is busted in two."

"And its one side is cracked," piped Fletcher.

"The two bottom shelves are okay," said Sam Jones, a quiet junior.

"If you just took the top and one side off, you could fix it. I think," said Spencer.

"Nah!" said Sam. "It's too late. You'd have to re-sand and re-varnish the whole thing after that, and it's the last day of school. It'd never dry by the time school's out. Hell…whoops." He looked sideways at Mr. Young, who didn't tolerate cussing in his class.

"Continue, Mr. Jones, without the gamey language, if you please."

"Well, what you'd have to do is take the top and the cracked side off, put new pieces on, sand it, varnish it, let it dry, sand it, varnish it again, and let it dry again. It'd take *days*."

"And we don't even got any wood cut that size," said Fletcher, in his high, nervous voice.

Eddie walked toward the table. He reached out his hand and touched the bookcase. The boys were silent.

"I was going to give it to my mother."

The boys looked at each other and then at the floor or out the windows. Fletcher sniffed and coughed.

"Well, let's get some wood cut at least," Spencer said.

✳   ✳   ✳   ✳

"Hey, did you hear?" Nancy hopped from one foot to another to keep warm.

"Hear what?" asked Spencer.

"That Len Dozier got expelled!"

"Good!"

"Right! You want to go to McDonald's with us?"

Spencer looked over her shoulder to Sally's Mustang.

"Nah, we got a shop project."

"A shop project!" Nancy stared in blank disbelief. "Spence. School's out," she said as if talking to a simple-minded child. She waved her hand in front of his face. "Wake up!"

"Yeah, well, we're helping somebody finish a project."

Nancy looked closely at Spencer. He wouldn't meet her eyes. "Okay," she said, puzzled. "See you later."

She could feel Spencer watching her cross the parking lot.

Sally turned up the radio. *"Help! I need somebody! Help! Not just anybody!"* The Beatles rang out over the parking lot. *"You know I need someone. Help!"*

Nancy looked back at Spencer. The look in his eyes gave her a chill of happiness. She smiled at him.

"Nancy!"

"What?"

"Want to go out Saturday night?"

A strand of her red-gold hair blew across her mouth. She pulled it out and said, "Sure."

Spencer grinned at her. "I'll call you," he said and then shivered and turned back to the shop building.

CHAPTER 13

▼

A MERRY LITTLE CHRISTMAS

Christmas morning Eddie woke up early. Some of the same Christmas feeling he'd had when he was a little boy made his heart beat faster. He flung back the covers, quickly grabbed a sweatshirt and pulled it on over his pajamas. His breath frosted in the cold of his bedroom. He could hear his mother in the kitchen, singing softly. She always tried to let them sleep as long as they could so she could wake them up to stacks of pancakes and bacon, their traditional Christmas breakfast.

He shoved his feet into his tennis shoes and slipped through the door out onto the back porch. He stopped outside the curtain to Lakeesha's bedroom and heard her soft breathing. He hardly dared to breathe himself as he opened the back door and stepped out into the cold morning. The rising sun sparkled in the frost on the grass. Eddie jogged down the street to Aunt Hattie's.

She bustled about in her kitchen, too, getting breakfast ready for her husband, Leonard, and son, Michael. She threw her fat arms around Eddie and gave him a loud kiss. He grimaced and then laughed and hugged her back.

"Here it is, boy. You be careful carrying it home, now. You don't want to hurt it."

Eddie laughed.

"Hush, hush, you wake them up." Hattie slapped his arm.

"Oh, Aunt Hattie, if you knew what this bookcase had gone through you wouldn't worry about it getting hurt."

Hattie opened the door, and Eddie carefully carried the bookcase through and down the middle of the soft dirt street. He tiptoed onto his porch, set the bookcase down, and looked through the window. A light from the kitchen made a big rectangle on the floor of the living room. His mother moved back and forth across the kitchen door.

Just then he saw Lakeesha come into the kitchen in her long night-gown. His father wouldn't be far behind. Eddie's hand slipped and hit the window. His mother looked into the living room in surprise and saw his face through the window. She came to the door and flung it open.

"Eddie, what are you doing out there in the cold?"

"I have your Christmas present." He picked up the bookcase and brought it into the living room. Eddie put the bookcase down in the space he had always reserved for it in his imagination.

"I made it for you." His mother stood in the doorway, the cold air blowing in.

"Oh, Eddie, how beautiful!" she breathed.

Lakeesha came to the kitchen door. "Oooh, there it is!"

His father looked over her shoulder. "Very handsome, son." He adjusted his glasses to see it better.

Eddie looked at his mother. She came to him with her arms outstretched and bundled him against her in a hard hug. When she let him go, her eyes were wet.

"Don't look at it too close, Mama. It's taken some hard knocks, but look at this." He turned it away from the wall. On the back in rough scrawls made with a wood-burning tool were the words,

"Merry Christmas, Mrs. Russell," and four names—Spencer Smith, Marvin Fletcher, Sam Jones, and Byron Young.

✳   ✳   ✳   ✳

Lethe sat on her bed in a long black crushed velvet dress with a white lace collar. Her round glasses reflected the colored lights she had strung up across her windows. Rochelle sat beside her, slim fingers busy in Lethe's thick hair.

Eddie, allowed into a girl's room as a special dispensation, stretched out on the deep window seat. Their parents were downstairs huddling with the men from the NAACP and SNCC and this time, a representative from the Southern Christian Leadership Conference. An Episcopalian minister, a white man, was also there.

"My hair won't grow this long," Rochelle said. "You should put a relaxer on it. You look like a little girl in these braids."

Lethe's house was in a fine black community that ran along the railroad tracks about a mile from their church. Big Victorian houses lined the short street; trees leaned over and shaded the sidewalk. The back yards were spacious. A store at the corner made fresh sandwiches wrapped in brown waxed paper and sold candy in big glass jars. The children had grown up loving that store, buying sour apple hard candy and gum drops.

Lethe's house had recently been painted white with fresh green shutters. The ceilings were tall, and the walls lined with books. Lethe's room had all the luxuries of white satin bedspreads and stuffed animals that any girl could want.

"What are they talking about?" asked Rochelle.

Eddie shrugged. "Said they were 'assessing the situation,' whatever that means."

"Be nice if they let us know what the 'situation' is," Rochelle said. "I think we might need to know something about it."

"I know one thing they're talking about," Lethe said. "They want you to play basketball, Eddie."

"Really? Nice of them to discuss it with me."

"You've always played basketball," Lakeesha said.

"Yeah, well, that's not the point."

"Don't you want to play?" Rochelle asked. "I wish they had a girls' team. I'd play for sure."

"Yeah, I want to play, but…Oh, I can't explain it. I feel like a prize bull or something. They just trot me out when they want something and expect me to go back to the barn and not complain."

"I wish we didn't ever have to go back to Forrest," Lakeesha said. She was curled on the floor, hugging one of Lethe's stuffed bears. "I want to go back to Douglass. It's just as good. But I can't let that Mrs. Granger win. I just can't."

She raised her voice a little to be heard over the yells of Lethe's little brother and sister, who were roaring up and down the hall outside with new Christmas toys.

"Come on, Lakeesha, we've been over and over this. It's getting boring," Eddie said. "We've got no choice. And besides I thought you'd decided on your own you were willing to go through with this, that day you fell down."

"I didn't 'fall down'," Lakeesha said, sulking.

"And Douglass certainly is *not* as good," Lethe said. "Forrest is a much better school. And it's got a chapter of the National Honor Society."

Rochelle snorted. "Hah! Just like they'd let you into the National Honor Society."

"I have the grades."

"You got better grades than anybody in the National Honor Society, honey. What you ain't got is the right color skin."

"I heard them talking about it, Lethe," Lakeesha said. "It's really hard to get in. They look at things like how many clubs you're in, and if you're a leader, and what church work you do, and…"

"And what color skin you got," Rochelle repeated.

Lakeesha glared at Rochelle. "Come on, Rochelle, it's more than that. Even white kids that make great grades don't get in the National

Honor Society unless they've done something more than just make good grades."

They looked at Lethe. Her lip stuck out. "I'm in the math club," she said.

"That ain't exactly leadership," Rochelle hooted.

"Well, I'm at Forrest, aren't I? Isn't that being a leader?" They all stared at her.

"I never thought of it that way," said Lakeesha.

"If you never thought of it that way, you can bet they won't think of it that way either," Eddie said.

Just then a car honked outside. Rochelle leaned over Eddie to look out the window.

"It's Clifford," she said. "Come on. Let's go see what he wants."

Eddie looked out the window over Rochelle's shoulder.

"Look at that old car the NAACP men have!" Rochelle said. "It's awful. Why do they have such a bad ride?"

"I know why they drive that old car," Lethe said. "Look at it. It's got those little tiny windows. That's so if anybody shoots at it, there's not such a big target."

"Oh, come on, Lethe," said Lakeesha, trying to see out over Eddie's shoulder.

"No, she's right. It's true," Eddie said.

Clifford honked again.

"Come on, let's go," said Rochelle, heading for the door.

Outside, Clifford leaned against the porch column with a big camera in his hand.

"Christmas!" He held it out for them to admire. "Let me take your picture. All of you. Line up!"

They lined up on the top step of the porch, Rochelle in the middle, one smaller girl under each arm, and Eddie crouched in front. They laughed, and Clifford snapped the picture. The flashbulb went off with a pop, blinding them for a moment on the soft, gray evening.

*   *   *   *

Nancy sat curled on the rug in her dark living room, next to the gleaming Christmas tree. She breathed in the scent of balsam. The colored lights glowed, and long tube lights bubbled with a hypnotic murmur. She touched her favorite ornament, one that had been her mother's when she was a little girl, a faded silver glass ball with two deep indentations, inside of which were lines of red, blue, green, gold.

She could hear her parents talking in the kitchen, ice clinking, glasses hitting each other with a clear chime. Company was coming. They sounded so contented, Nancy thought. She wanted to be a child again, when just to gaze into the tree was wonder enough.

The doorbell rang. "I'll get it." She ran to open the door, a gust of cold air blew in. "Hi, Spence."

"Hey!"

Her father stepped out of the kitchen, examining Spencer. He held out his hand; Spencer took it easily.

"Liked that last block of yours in the West Side game," he said.

Spencer beamed. "Yeah, that was pretty great, wasn't it?" Then he laughed and blushed. "Not me, I mean, it was a great ending, wasn't it?"

They were limbering up to talk football endlessly. "No, no!" Nancy yanked on Spencer's coat sleeve. "Don't start on football. We'll never get out of here if you do."

"Home by eleven, Nan."

"You got it, Mr. Martin." Spencer held the door for Nancy, who had spun into her coat.

"Let's go to the Pig and Whistle," Spencer said as he opened the car door for her.

They drove downtown, talking and playing the radio, but Nancy felt the frozen nervousness she always felt on a first date, even though it was just Spencer. Every word seemed to fall out of her mouth and hang in the air, unnatural and obvious. The car isolated them in the dark night, a metal capsule speeding down Bellevue Boulevard. Even though she and Spencer had been friends since kindergarten, had danced together for years, hands locked together and arms twined around each other's waists, they'd never been alone together.

Spencer turned the knob on the radio. Christmas music filled the space between them with sound, and Nancy relaxed. Her head fell back on the seat.

Nancy had a sudden feeling of freedom, as if she were grown, flying home through the night to some snow-bound New England farm. The song ended just as they pulled into the parking lot of the Pig and Whistle, a whitewashed, half-timbered barbecue restaurant.

When they got out, a high voice chimed across the dark parking lot. "Well, look who's here!"

Spencer whirled around. Nancy stopped halfway out of the car, as if she'd been tagged playing statues. "Oh, foot," she said.

The door of a long, black limousine opened, and Maryanne's narrow face with the perfect cap of dark blond hair peered out. Then she almost fell out of the car, and a masculine arm shot out and caught the back of her sweater. Maryanne laughed sloppily and waved her arms around, hanging out of the car door.

"Spencer, what are you doing with my girl?" Larry asked.

"I am not your girl." Nancy stepped out of the car.

Spencer looked confused. Maurice, Maryanne's black chauffeur, sat in the front seat, staring sideways at them, a half-smile on his face.

"Oh, forget her, Larry," Maryanne said. "I'm your girlfriend now. Y'all come have a drink with us. Maurice got it for us."

She waved a fifth of Jack Daniels at them.

Nancy grabbed Spencer's hand and pulled hard. "Let's go," she whispered.

Spencer looked reluctantly at the waving bottle of whiskey and followed Nancy into the restaurant. As the door closed, Larry shouted something, and Maryanne screamed something back at him. The black Lincoln revved its engine, and the door slammed. Nancy looked through the stained glass windows of the entrance to the Pig and

Whistle and watched the car ease out on to Union. Her shoulders dropped, and she breathed deep, her eyes closed.

When she opened her eyes, Spencer was looking at her, his forehead wrinkled. His mouth quirked up to one side. He shook his head.

"What?" she asked.

"Nothing." He put his hand on her shoulder. "Let's go get some barbecue."

Inside it was dark and quiet. The black waiter greeted them by name since they came there with a gang of kids nearly every weekend. They didn't see anyone they knew and slid into a wooden booth, facing each other.

"So, Nan, you don't still like that creep, do you?"

Nancy stared at him. "Larry?"

"Ummm," said Spencer, looking down at his menu.

She ran her hand over the smooth, varnished wood. "I hate him," she whispered.

"You do?"

She looked up at Spencer's plump face. His cheeks were pink, and his brown eyes were so familiar. This was her friend, her old friend. She took a breath that shivered in her chest.

"If I tell you something, do you swear not to tell anyone else?"

"Sure," he said.

"I was never going to tell anybody about this. My parents are the only ones who know. He hit me." Nancy ran her finger over a little scar under her hair right at the edge of her forehead over her left eye.

Spencer's mouth dropped open, then he quickly shut it. His jaw twitched.

"He was always after me to—go all the way," she said in a rush. "And I wanted to break up with him, but when I told him I didn't want to go out with him anymore, he hit me, a lot…Daddy wanted to have him arrested, but Mother talked him out of it. Now he won't leave me alone. He's apologized a million times. He calls at 2 a.m., and keeps calling and calling. Daddy had to change our number. He throws beer cans in my yard. He stares at me. You've seen him. He's always watching me. I hate him."

She put her face in her hands, felt something move in her chest like a sheet of ice breaking up. Spencer reached out and put his hand around her wrist, then stroked her hair.

"You want me to kill him for you?" Spencer asked.

Nancy looked up, unable to laugh yet, but Spencer wasn't laughing either.

"No, no, surely he'll stop hounding me, eventually."

∗   ∗   ∗   ∗

"Come in and look at my Christmas tree," Nancy said as they pulled into her driveway.

"Okay," he said.

They ran across the frozen yard and through the front door into the dark living room. The twinkling lights on the tree sparkled on the windows, on the tiles around the mantelpiece, the mirror over the sideboard, the glass over the pictures.

Spencer reached out and touched Nancy's cheek. She was as still as a statue. He leaned down and kissed her. His lips were soft and hard at the same time, not slobbery kisses like that awful time she'd gone parking with Bobby Davidson. She closed her eyes but she couldn't respond to his kiss.

Spencer dropped his hand and stepped back. She felt bereft, wanted to fall against his chest like falling onto bed at night when she was really tired.

"Goodnight, Nancy."

"Goodnight, Spence. I had a good time."

He moved toward the door slowly. "Yeah, so did I." He closed the door behind him.

Nancy raced for the door and yanked it open. "Spence!"

He turned around.

"Keep asking me out. Please?"

"Sure," he said. "How about Friday?"

"Yes!" She slammed the door, leaned against the closed door and listened until she heard his car start. *What am I up to with him?"* she thought.

The red tail lights disappeared up the dark road. Nancy stepped out on the porch and looked up at the stars in the black sky, trapped in a net of tree branches. She puffed out a breath, shining in the starlight. She thought of Eddie and Lakeesha, wondered what their Christmas had been like. Then she remembered those voices from the boys' bathroom. Nancy went inside and carefully locked the door, then into the kitchen to make sure the back door was locked.

▼

CHAPTER 14

DON'T STAND IN THE DOORWAYS, DON'T BLOCK UP THE HALLS

"Here's the list!" Missy waved a mimeographed sheet of paper.

Nancy, Kathy Perkins and April Rawlins, the National Honor Society Tapping Ceremony Committee, all grabbed for it. Missy laid the paper on the library table, and they huddled together to look.

"Oh, oh, fantastic! Sally's getting in this time," Nancy squealed.

"And Lynn Monahan, that's good," said Kathy.

"Lethe Jefferson!" gasped April.

"What! They can't!" Kathy grabbed at the paper. Missy snatched it away.

"They can. They have. Now what are we going to do about it? I've already matched up who I think should tap who, but we need to discuss who's going to tap this colored girl."

"Can't we do anything about it?" squeaked Kathy.

Miss Thoreau banged into the library. "Hah, what's up?"

"We are discussing the Honor Society induction ceremony," Missy said.

"What's the problem? You all look ready to spit nails at each other."

"We're discussing how we're going to tap Lethe Jefferson," Missy said through clenched teeth.

"Oh, ho, so that's the problem. Hah! Shame it's a problem, but there you go." Miss Thoreau slammed the door.

"That tall, skinny one's a pet of hers, isn't she?" asked Missy.

"You mean Rochelle?" Nancy asked.

Missy ignored the edge in Nancy's voice.

"Oh, yes!" said Kathy. "It's sickening, really."

"She's come a long way for the daughter of a garbage man, oh, excuse me, 'sanitation worker,'" mocked Missy. "And her Daddy is a union shop steward, no less."

"She writes fine essays." April looked over her glasses at the others.

"For a Negro?" asked Missy.

"For a high school junior." April glanced at Nancy.

"Oh, now I guess you'll be suggesting we induct *her* into the Honor Society," said Missy.

"No, she doesn't have the grades."

"I don't know what we're accomplishing by inducting that girl into the Honor Society," said Kathy. "It will just draw attention to them, and they are much better off ignored, believe me."

"I think being ignored is about the cruelest thing of all," said Nancy. "I'd rather have someone insult me than ignore me. If they insulted me, then I could fight back."

"That's all we need. Race wars in our hallways," said Missy.

Nancy was silent, a red spot of anger on each cheek. She looked at April, who was looking down at her Honor Society notebook, a little twitch in her jaw.

"You know, I've always been convinced that this Lethe is cheating," said Kathy.

"Why do you say that?" asked Nancy.

"Well, my little brother is in geometry with her, and her grades are perfect. Every one. Perfect. Never one single mistake. She has to be cheating! No one else makes perfect scores. And that's what they can't figure out. If she's cheating, who is she cheating off of? She must have the answers somewhere, but they just can't catch her at it."

April snorted. "Kathy, I hate to burst your little bubble, but that girl's not cheating. Her father is a professor of mathematics at Memphis State. He's got a Ph.D. from the University of Chicago and a B.A. from Oberlin. That's a darned sight better degree than any of our teachers have and better schools than any of them went to."

They stared at April, stunned. Fuming, Nancy thought of Lethe's face, the determined chin, the stubborn mouth, the precise speech, her finger marking the place in a book. How could anyone think for one minute that she would cheat?

"This is pointless," said Missy. "We're going to induct her. We have to. She's got the grades, and the teachers have decided she has the leadership. If we don't, we'll look like…"

They all understood. Nancy decided to say it anyway. "We'll look like we're bigots?" She exchanged a glance with April.

"I don't want to do it," Kathy said.

"I'm happy to do it," Nancy said. "It would be an honor."

"I want to do it too. Shall we thumb-wrestle for it, Nancy?" asked April. They laughed.

"Absolutely not!" Missy practically spit at April and Nancy. "I have it all planned. Nancy, you have to tap Sally, you've been friends forever, and April, I have you down to tap Stephen Gatson. Kathy, you are going to tap that Lethe Jefferson, so that's it. And Nancy, I simply do not understand your attitude. April's one thing, but you?"

"What? April's always been weird, but you counted on me to toe the line? Is that it, Missy?"

They glared at each other.

"Oh, please, don't let's fight," Kathy pleaded. "I guess I'll have to do it. Just go on, tell us what to do."

Missy took a deep breath. "Okay. All right. Here's how it goes. We start on stage with unlit candles…"

∗   ∗   ∗   ∗

In the darkened auditorium, Honor Society members with lit candles began to move off the stage and then up and down the aisles. Slowly, they moved from the aisles down the rows of seats, tapping a shoulder here, a shoulder there. A rustle would move outward, and a student would rise and follow the candle to the stage.

In the balcony, Eddie and Rochelle had managed to get seats behind Lethe and Lakeesha. Eddie saw Lethe's hands grip the arms of the seat. The candles moved into their area. A student was tapped two rows ahead of them, and then the candles moved out of the balcony. Lethe breathed in hard, and then was still as stone. A murmur ran through the rows around them.

Minutes passed in silence as candles led the tapped students onto the stage. They gathered in a straggling row and faced the audience. Then there was a flurry on the stage. Miss Cross, the Honor Society sponsor, stood face-to-face with someone who was shaking her head. Then the figure lit its candle. The candle bobbed down the steps, up the aisle, disappeared at the back, then reappeared in the balcony, coming straight to Lethe's row.

Hands trembling so hard the candle nearly went out, Kathy Perkins reached in and tapped Lethe on the shoulder. For a long moment Lethe was motionless in her seat. Everyone in the dark auditorium breathed in. Eddie leaned forward. "Go!" he whispered in her ear.

Lethe stood and followed Kathy down the aisle, out the back of the auditorium balcony; she reappeared walking down the long aisle to the stage. On the stage, Lethe slowly moved to join the small group of sophomores and juniors who had just been tapped. She stood just slightly away from them. Eddie crossed his arms across his chest. Lakeesha, glancing back at him, clapped her hands together, but made no sound until everyone in the auditorium began to applaud. Then she clapped hard.

Eddie didn't. That girl, Kathy Perkins, from his English class, that one that was going out with the class president. He'd thought she was all right. She wasn't. She'd ruined Lethe's moment. He couldn't get above it, and slumped in his seat, eyes closed.

*   *   *   *

Nancy rushed down the hallway, late for English class, fuming, wanting to stamp her feet and scream, strangle Kathy. She'd ruined everything, for everyone, made the whole thing ridiculous. And then had the gall to insist she had been "taking a stand." Nancy strangled down a cuss word, bit it back hard, but she wished she could go into the field behind her house and scream, like she did sometimes when she was furious with her parents or Sally or after Larry…

A sharp voice made Nancy stop and listen. "Well, this is the last straw!"

Nancy leaned back and looked around the corner.

"They don't know where to stop," said Kinsey Mackay. "I'm just not going to take it anymore. Len will show them once and for all what's what. There's people at this school who aren't afraid to stand up, either."

"What, Kinsey? What's he going to do?" asked Lucille Jones, one of Kinsey's gang.

"You wait. He's got friends now he's out of school—because of those coloreds." She stopped, her face red and splotched. "They're as fed up as we are with the way things are going, and they're not afraid to do something about it."

"But what?" asked Rosie Belew.

"Who?" asked Lucille.

"I said, you wait. I'll tell you when I'm damned good and ready." Kinsey marched off down the hall, her short red hair bouncing like a doll's.

Nancy bit her lip and leaned back against the wall. Then she heard Kinsey's shrill voice hiss, "Snowflake, snowflake."

Nancy peeked around the corner. Lakeesha and Rochelle were walking together down the hall. Rochelle stopped, but Lakeesha hurried on, until Rochelle caught her arm and jerked her to a halt. Rochelle stood for a moment, silent, her head down. The voice came again. "Snow*flake*, snow*flake*," with a nasty shift in emphasis.

Rochelle spun around. Kinsey Mackay was about twenty feet behind them, surrounded by her friends. They all grinned. Rochelle looked over their heads and caught Nancy's eye, but Kinsey and her friends were focused on Lakeesha and didn't notice that Nancy was behind them.

Rochelle marched forward, dragging Lakeesha by the arm. She stopped about two feet away from Kinsey and stared at her. Kinsey's grin faded.

"Who are you calling Snowflake, Charcoal?" Rochelle snapped, so savagely that Kinsey backed up, stepping on Rosie's toe.

Oooh, how perfect! Nancy thought.

"Ouch," Rosie screeched and pushed Kinsey, hard.

Kinsey pushed her back, then stepped up into Rochelle's face. "I'm calling your little friend there Snowflake. You want to stop me?"

"Yeah, Charcoal, I'll stop you."

"Stop, Rochelle, you'll get us in trouble." Lakeesha grabbed her arm. Rochelle shook her off.

The girls faced off, and a crowd began to circle them.

"Rochelle, you'll get us kicked out of school," Lakeesha pleaded.

Kinsey smiled. "That's just what we want, isn't it? We want you colored girls out of *our* school."

Rochelle took one step forward, and at that moment, Nancy moved, shoving herself between them.

"Really, Kinsey?" Nancy said. "Is that what you want? Why don't you pick on me? It would take a lot to get *me* kicked out of this school." Nancy stepped forward until she was nose-to-nose with Kinsey.

"Oh, here comes the nigger-lover to protect her little friends," Kinsey hissed.

"What do you mean by that, Kinsey?" Nancy took another step forward, and Kinsey backed up. "Do you mean that I think these girls are nice, that I like them, that I respect them more than I do a vicious cat like you? Well, you're right. And so is Rochelle. Charcoal's a good name for you. You're small."

She took another step forward. "And dark."

Another step. "And dirty."

Another step. Now Kinsey was backed up against the hot radiator.

"Stop, Nancy," Lakeesha said in the sudden silence.

Nancy stopped and looked Kinsey up and down. She turned and stalked off.

*   *   *   *

After school, Eddie and his father pulled into the service station where they had bought their gas for fifteen years. Reverend Russell stopped the old green Buick in front of the pump and got out of the car.

Len Dozier slouched out of the office, stopping dead in his tracks when he saw Reverend Russell. His face hardened even more when he looked into the car and recognized Eddie.

Len stood up straighter and swaggered toward them.

"We don't sell gas to you people," he said shrilly.

"That's strange, son, because I've bought my gasoline here for as long as I've owned a car."

"Yeah, well, we don't sell to coloreds no more."

Eddie slowly got out of the car. He stood up straight, looming taller than his father, much taller than Len. He lowered his head and looked hard at Len, his eyes smoldering.

"That's right. Don't sell to no coloreds." Len nodded his head, not meeting either Eddie or Reverend Russell's eyes.

Eddie took another step forward. His father put a hand on the sleeve of his jacket.

A huge man emerged from the office, obese folds of flesh quavering. Len spun around.

"You want to repeat what I just heard you say?" Billy Blystone said to Len.

"I told 'em we don't sell to coloreds," Len said, still defiant but less sure of himself.

"Maybe you don't, boy, but I do, so pump Reverend Russell's gas." Blystone's voice was a deep roar.

"Damned if I will," Len muttered.

"Then get on out of here. Take your coat and git."

Len looked from his employer to Reverend Russell to Eddie, trapped. In a sudden fury, he flung the oily rag in his hand onto the cracked concrete. "*God*-damned niggers!"

He marched into the station, cussing every step of the way. "Damn it to hell! Always something! Just because I stand up to them! Ruining everything!" Then they couldn't hear him anymore. A car door slammed and from the back of the station they heard an unmuffled motor start up. Len's rusted Chevy screeched around the corner and shot off down the highway with a gout of blue exhaust fumes.

"First day on the job." Blystone shook his head. "Shouldn't of hired him. Had a bad feeling but…Well, it's hard to get help at all." He shook his head again, sighed and unhooked the gas pump.

"So, Reverend, shall I fill 'er up?"

Eddie leaned against the hood of the car, breathing in the gasoline fumes. Blystone hummed to himself at the other end of their car.

"Dad, I can't do it," he said.

"Do what, son?"

"Find anything in Len Dozier to love."

Reverend Russell glanced back at the white man and stepped closer to Eddie. "Love often does not come easily. It comes first from understanding. That young man has probably had a hard and loveless life. He needs desperately to feel that someone in the world is inferior to him. He's always had the comfort of thinking everyone may despise him but at least he's a step above the 'niggers.' You shatter that fantasy, Eddie. He's bound to hate you and all the rest of us."

Eddie looked at his feet.

"You may be right, but it's a tall order, trying to love that piece of dirt," laughed Blystone, clicking the pump handle to top off the tank.

Reverend Russell permitted himself a small smile.

"I can understand it in my head, but I can't feel it," Eddie said. *And neither can you,* he thought.

CHAPTER 15

▼

TALKING TRASH

Townsend's so stupid! So slow! He can't play basketball worth a damn. Why doesn't he follow through? He's tall, but he won't jump; he couldn't dunk to save his life. Never takes a shot unless it's completely safe.

Eddie sweated, dribbling the ball down the court, slowly, looking for Townsend. He was having a bad night. Every time he had the ball, all the fans in Woodson's seats went, "Huh, huh, huh," like gorillas and scratched their sides.

"Huh, huh, huh," they grunted in unison.

Eddie ducked around a Woodson guard and dribbled back to half-court. Townsend was open in the corner. Coach Humphrey had told Eddie to get Townsend the ball.

Eddie bounced the ball, his eyes locked with Townsend's. He should pass him the ball, but he was so stupid, so slow. He was also open in three-point range. Eddie tensed to pass, but Townsend waved his arms, asking for the ball. Instantly Woodson had two guards on him. The moment of opportunity passed. *So slow, so stupid. He couldn't have made that shot even if I'd gotten him the ball.*

"Huh, huh, huh!"

Eddie's lips twitched. He shot down the court, dodging surprised Woodson players. Townsend was right in front of him.

"You slow-assed, Townsend," Eddie said, his face close to Townsend's so no one else could hear.

He darted around the astounded Townsend, into the paint, leaped skyward, and dunked the ball with a shout. He came down to the floor like a feather, his head filled with light. He raised his fist, and in the Forrest stands, his fans, his own fans, his friends and family from Douglass, screamed his name. The ball came down out of the basket into his hands.

Woodson threw the ball in, Eddie pressed until they passed half-court. He then went into zone defense, stopped a shot and then the Woodson player was past him into the paint, where Townsend stood like a stump, watching the player go up and roll the ball gently into the basket.

*   *   *   *

Nancy spun on the hard gym floor, the pleats of her royal blue skirt flaring. The gold lining flashed.

> *Basket, basket, basket, boys.*
> *You make the basket,*
> *We'll make the noise.*

Out on the court, Forrest was down by two. Their basketball season had been mediocre, and this game against Woodson High, a basketball powerhouse, was rough.

Nancy looked at the clock. The gym was hot and bright, not like being out in the autumn wind under the stars for football.

"Huh, huh, huh," the Woodson fans chanted.

"I can't stand that 'huh-huh' thing much longer," Nancy said to Sally.

Sally wiped her forehead and nodded.

A Woodson player caught the inbound pass, dribbled down court, shot, missed. Townsend took it out, passed it in to Eddie. Eddie came down the court with the ball, a steady dribble, good foot work. He stopped, faked a pass, then darted around his opponent and sped down the court.

"Huh, huh, huh!"

He passed to Townsend. Townsend shot and missed. The Forrest crowd groaned.

Spencer grabbed the rebound, shot, missed. A louder groan from the fans, especially from the small group of black fans at the far end of the bleachers. Eddie's friends and family came to every home game. Nancy looked over their faces. Rochelle had brought Clifford, Vernell was there. Coach Frazier sat next to Reverend Russell. Other faces she didn't recognize. They all cheered passionately for Eddie. No other player had such a loyal and loud following. No other player was half as good as Eddie, either. They were much more excited about this game than she was.

"Spence shouldn't shoot," Cindy said. "He's a great rebounder, but his shooting stinks."

"So does Larry's, actually," Sally said.

A whistle shrilled. Woodson's guard had chopped Spencer's arm, and Spencer would go to the foul line.

Nancy beat her pom-poms together. Spencer slowly bounced the ball, the beginning of his tedious foul shooting ritual. Eddie and Townsend stood across from each other. Suddenly Townsend stood up and started across the paint toward Eddie.

Bobby Davidson grabbed Townsend's arm, and Townsend moved back, but he and Eddie continued to glare at each other.

Just as Spencer finally shot, a crash echoed from outside the gym. The cheerleaders spun toward the sound. Another crash resounded. The players faltered. Forrest's coach, Jerry Humphrey, called a time out. A referee stuck his head out the door under the goal and quickly pulled it back in.

Another crash and angry shouts. A few fans jumped up and ran to the doors to look out. A final crash, then Nancy heard tires squealing. She followed Missy at a run to the door. All the glass in the four big glass doors of the gym was broken. Missy took a cautious step forward and with two fingers carefully pulled a yellow piece of paper off a brick. She unfolded it. Bold black writing: "Be a Man, Join the Klan."

Coach Humphrey loomed up beside Missy and grabbed the paper. He taught Modern History and laughed a lot, but he wasn't laughing now. Nancy backed into the gym and ran to where the cheerleaders were lining up for a cheer.

"Larry, Larry, *he's* our man," Missy dipped and swooshed her pom-poms across the floor by her feet and then stood. "If he can't do it." She turned and made an L of her arms, pointing to Nancy.

"Eddie, can!" Nancy shouted. She had agreed at the beginning of the season to take Eddie's name in this cheer, because the other girls didn't want to. "Eddie, Eddie, *he's* our man…"

They tried to get the crowd's attention, but it was useless. The two teams huddled anxiously on their benches. The refs huddled in the middle of the court. The fans huddled in the stands, the group of Negroes as far away from the whites as possible. No one paid any attention to the cheerleaders, and eventually they, too, huddled at the edge of the court.

Finally, they heard the wail of sirens.

"Fat lot of good those cops are going to do now," Sally said.

The two coaches came back in. A ref whirled his arm and blew his whistle. From the lobby Nancy could hear the squawk of two-way radios and the rhythmic scrape of someone sweeping up glass.

When play resumed, Eddie's hands trembled. Everything that had happened shrank to a pinpoint, and on the head of the pin Larry Townsend danced, mocking him with that smug grin.

A loud whistle cut across his progress down the court. A mean-looking ref with the whistle in his mouth rolled his hands.

Traveling?

The fans jumped to their feet, screaming protest.

"No way!" Eddie yelled at the ref.

A twisted smile split the ref's thin face. He chopped his hands together in a T.

Technical foul?

"Noooo!" screamed the crowd.

Eddie slammed the basketball onto the court.

The ref laughed. He jerked his thumb at the sidelines. *Ejected?*

"Noooo!!" screamed the fans.

Eddie leaped toward the ref, but Spencer had one of his moments of blinding speed. He caught Eddie in his arms and wrestled him to the sidelines.

Coach Humphrey's sad blue eyes locked with Eddie's furious dark ones. Eddie's fury popped like a balloon.

"Sorry, Coach," he muttered.

"Go on to the locker room, Eddie."

Eddie began the lonely walk down the sidelines. A whistle blew. Play resumed.

The chaos in the bleachers continued. All the black young people were still on their feet, screaming. They began to chant, "Ed-die! Ed-die! Ed-die!"

The ref was talking to Coach Humphrey and pointing up at the screaming black crowd. Coach looked up at them and waved his arms up and down, telling them to quiet down.

"Sit down," a burly man in a Forrest jacket yelled at them. "You're going to get us a T."

"Oh, yeah, that ref is a…" Rochelle yelled, cut off by Coach Frazier grabbing her by the arm.

"Sit down," the burly man yelled at Rochelle, and white fans all over the stands picked up the chant.

"Sit down, sit down," they yelled at the group of Negroes.

"What is going on?" Nancy asked.

"They're just acting the way they usually act," Missy said, her freckled face pale.

"What do they expect? He traveled! They don't think he should get called for it?" Cindy said.

"He did not travel! It was a bad call!" Nancy said.

"Oh, Nancy, you don't know anything about basketball," Sally said.

"Well, I don't know if he traveled or not, but he did throw that ball at the ref, and you can't do that and get away with it," Missy said.

"Yeah, but he was—"

A body brushed her. Rochelle swept by, followed by the crowd of Douglass students. The cheerleaders squeezed back against the railing as the scowling Negroes pushed by.

Someone shouted, "Get out!" The entire white crowd took up the chant. "Get out! Get out!" The chant followed the Douglass kids as they marched out of the gym, heads high. As they went through the door, Rochelle raised her clenched fist. Then all the Douglass students shot their fists in the air as they disappeared through the door and down the stairs.

Coach Frazier stood, leaning down to speak urgently to Reverend Russell, who shook his head, lips pressed tightly together. Coach Frazier shrugged and followed the students out of the gym, a few shouts of "Get out!" chasing him.

Nancy watched Reverend Russell. He sat in his usual silent dignity, Lakeesha huddled at his side. Missy started a cheer. Nancy didn't move. Sally poked her in the back. Still she didn't move. She looked toward the door, at Coach Frazier's broad shoulders filling the space and then disappearing.

Nancy turned back to the court. The game was a washout. Forrest now trailed by twelve points, with less than a minute to go. With mutters of disgust, the white fans began to leave as well.

The cheerleaders bounced up and down and waved their arms meaninglessly, pom-poms shimmering gold. They looked so weird. Nancy stood unmoving on the edge of the shining basketball court. The cheerleaders stared at her, their eyes as blank as dolls. She couldn't move.

Sally shook Nancy's arm. "What's the matter?"

Nancy shook her head. "Nothing seems real," she said.

The final buzzer blew. Only the cheerleaders and Reverend Russell and Lakeesha were still in the Forrest stands. Over in the Woodson bleachers, a jubilant crowd was beginning to move toward the doors and their cars and buses waiting outside the gym.

*   *   *   *

Eddie sat in the locker room with his head in his hands. His chest hurt, and his stomach knotted.

He had lost control. He had let his father down, let his people down. He had let his team down, his coach. Both Coach Humphrey, who he really liked, and Coach Frazier, who had been up there watching him play. He clenched his fists and pounded them on his trembling thighs. He had totally abandoned himself to his hatred of Townsend, and had gone after him with the son-of-a-bitch's own tool kit—sneering, mocking, taunting, trying to humiliate him with the truth, rub his face in the dirt.

Slow, stupid. Can't hold that ball? Can't hit that shot, huh, big guy? What? A little slow? How about stupid? How about can't play basketball for shit? He'd been gigging Townsend like that all night. The worst thing was that it hadn't even made him feel better. It hadn't changed a thing, except to get him thrown out of the game. He still hated Townsend with a visceral loathing that nothing would ever change. But acting on it had blown up in his face, burning like acid.

He heard footsteps and voices, and the door banged open. He looked up, his eyes tortured. Coach was the first one in. He stopped just inside the door, the players jostling behind him.

"Come with me, Eddie." He headed for his little office across the hall. Eddie followed, miserably.

"Bye-bye, blackbird," Townsend sang as Eddie passed.

Eddie stopped. His head shot up, his hate raced back, flooding him with energy.

Spencer put a hand on Townsend's arm. "Cut it out, Townsend."

"I'll get to you later, Larry," Coach said. "Don't leave until we talk."

He turned and walked out, Eddie at his heels. Once in the office, Coach sank into the ripped swivel chair in his office with a huge sigh. He leaned his head back and massaged the bridge of his nose. "Ugh, I'm tired."

Eddie watched him warily.

Coach sat up, the chair creaked and wobbled. "So, Eddie, what do you think about what happened tonight?"

Eddie looked at his basketball shoes. His blue nylon basketball shorts stuck to his legs. "It's my fault, Coach. It's all my fault. Even what those men did, those bricks..." Eddie's hands clenched, his voice broke.

"Maybe it wouldn't have happened if you hadn't been here," Coach said. "But don't get confused about things. Those men are responsible for what they did tonight, Eddie, not you."

"But I lost it, Coach. I just completely lost it tonight."

To his surprise, Coach chuckled. "I was wondering when you would, Eddie. You need to lose your temper, son. It ain't natural not to. It's just a shame you got a T for it. That's because you're colored, of course. Another player, they wouldn't have done a thing."

Eddie stared at Coach Humphrey, who laughed again at his expression.

"You think I don't know how stupid Townsend is? How slow? I don't blame you for losing your cool with him. It's time somebody did. Everybody thinks he's so damned great. He needs to be brought down a bit. Glad you did it."

"I don't think I really got to him, Coach. He just thinks I'm a nig—"

"Don't say it." Coach held his hand up. "Don't think it either. You're a better basketball player than he is. That's what's eating him, though he'll never admit it."

Eddie felt his mouth hanging open, closed it.

"Emotion's not such a terrible thing, Eddie. You have too much, and I don't want to see it bust out like that again, but I'm not angry with you about it. There's a lot of trash talk in basketball. It's part of the game."

"Coach, my father—"

"You have to be your own person, Eddie, find your own way of dealing with things. Most of the team knows you're good, respects you. You could be a leader on this team. You lost your temper, fine, you'll play looser now. Go on, Eddie. Take your shower, and send that dumb ass Townsend in here."

Eddie walked thoughtfully back to the locker room. Most of the players were nearly dressed. Eddie went down the aisle where his locker was, between Townsend's and Spencer's.

"Where is he?" Eddie asked Spencer.

"Already gone."

CHAPTER 16

▼

NIGHT RIDE

Nancy and Sally hurried down the stairs to the sidewalk heading for Sally's car, which was parked on a side street behind the gym. In the dark parking lot, the Woodson team was milling around their humming bus. Some boys were getting on, but most of them were just hanging around outside of it, laughing. One shouted "losers" at them, and they quickened their pace.

As they turned the corner, Nancy saw Lakeesha standing under a streetlight that cast harsh shadows across her face. "Hi," Nancy said. "Need a ride home?" She felt Sally stiffen by her side.

"No, I'm just waiting for Daddy to bring the car around," Lakeesha said, not meeting Nancy's eyes.

Nancy glanced over her shoulder. She couldn't see the doors to the gym anymore, or the Woodson boys and their bus. In fact, she couldn't see anyone else.

"Okay," Nancy said. "See you later." She followed Sally down the sidewalk. Sally opened the door of the Mustang and slid in. Nancy was opening the door when she heard the unmuffled roar of a car out on the highway. Her heart sped up. Surely they weren't coming back, those men with the bricks.

Nancy stood on the sidewalk, waiting for Sally to lean across and unlock the door for her. Lakeesha stood a few yards away, alone under the streetlight.

The roar came closer. Headlights turned the corner from the highway onto the street where Lakeesha and Nancy stood. They looked at each other and then turned in unison to look toward the headlights.

Nancy saw a long stick emerge from the window of the oncoming car. The engine roared, and the car leaped forward.

Nancy froze in space and time. Her mind floated somewhere just above her motionless body. "Broom handle," Nancy thought calmly, seeing it move in exquisite slow motion toward Lakeesha. That second stretched out like a rubber band, hours long. A brilliant flash of light made Nancy blink. Then the broom handle hit Lakeesha with an awful crack. Nancy heard it even over the growling car that sped toward her and the ugly shouting from inside it.

The stick disappeared inside the window. Another flash of light came from somewhere behind her. The car swerved. Nancy came back to life and ducked as it shot past her. She caught a glimpse of Len Dozier's face in the front window and a pale face framed with bushy red hair in the back—Kinsey Mackay. Someone else was in the front seat, driving the car. Someone who looked familiar, but it was too quick, too dark. The car sped off down the side street, burning rubber down past the football field, skidding from side to side.

Legs trembling, Nancy pushed herself against terrible fear toward Lakeesha's still body, stopping by her side. The white light of the streetlamp glared down on Lakeesha's face. Something had happened to it. Blood leaked down from a deep dent across her eyes and nose. Nancy couldn't look, her eyes slipped away, her stomach heaved, and she found herself looking down on the sidewalk, recognizing the dark stain as blood. Someone was by her side. She looked up. It was Clifford with a box camera in his hands.

"Oh, God help us," he said.

Nancy whirled around, bending forward. "Sally, Sally!" Nancy screamed. "Go get somebody. Go *get* somebody."

Sally's face was a white blur through the windshield of the Mustang. She didn't move. The door didn't open.

Nancy knelt down next to Lakeesha, said her name, touched her cheek. It felt cold, damp with blood. An old green car pulled up next to her, and Reverend Russell jumped out, moving faster than Nancy had ever imagined he could. He was by her side, kneeling next to her. He picked up Lakeesha's limp hand and held it in both of his. "Lakeesha, Lakeesha," he called softly. Lakeesha could not answer.

Nancy jumped up. "I'll go get help," she said. She tore off around the corner and back to the door of the gym. The Woodson boys still hadn't gotten on the bus. Their faces looked like white balloons with black eyes painted on. People were coming out the door from the gym. Eddie! She ran toward him, flung herself at him.

Eddie had just pushed the bar on the gym door and stepped out into the damp February night. A piece of glass crunched under his foot. Someone had already put up brown paper to cover the broken windows. He was on his way to the corner to meet Lakeesha, who would be waiting as usual for their father to bring the car around. Reverend Russell always parked a good distance from the gym. It was part of his overall confrontation/non-confrontation strategy, in general not to presume too much, not to walk to his car with all the white people, open the doors right next to them and drive away just like he was one of the crowd. Eddie's father carefully chose his battles, and some things he simply avoided.

Eddie was aware of the Woodson team off to the side, their bus growling, the boys looking at the Forrest team, confident and cocky in their victory. Eddie saw Nancy Martin running toward them, up the stairs to the doors of the gym, where the team all clustered, just released by Coach Humphrey. She was running strangely, her hands held out in front of her. She came closer and Eddie saw her face, pale and twisted. He stopped. They all stopped. Nancy ran straight at him, grabbed him, touched his chest, gripped his jacket. He tried to step back, but she held him harder, switching her hold from his jacket to his shirt. Eddie felt a stir through the crowd of boys around him.

Eddie glanced from side to side. The entire Woodson team seemed to be fascinated by the sight of a white cheerleader clutching a Negro. Eddie stepped back again, but Nancy moved with him.

She found her voice and gasped. "Eddie, Eddie, Lakeesha. Come on. Hurry."

Eddie was frozen, looking at her, his eyes wide. He looked down at his shirt. Where she'd grabbed it, she'd left dark stains.

Other bodies came up around them.

Spencer was there. "What's wrong?" he asked.

"Go get help!" Nancy whirled at Spencer, pushing her sticky hands at his chest. "Call an ambulance. Call the police. Lakeesha's hurt. I saw it. It's bad, it's bad. Please, Spence. Get help."

Spencer turned and ran back inside the gym. Nancy pulled at Eddie's hand, and he followed her down the gym steps to the sidewalk. Then they were both running. Eddie could see his father bending over something on the sidewalk. Lakeesha. He sped up, dropping Nancy's hand. He heard Coach Humphrey's voice behind him, barking something. Then he was at Lakeesha's side, kneeling beside her, beside his father, who was shaking, holding her hand. Eddie realized his father was crying, although no sound escaped him. He looked down at his sister's broken face, her nose smashed, her eyes blood-filled, realized the stain on the sidewalk was blood. He knelt on the sidewalk beside his father, beside his sister, and bent his head, choking back screams of fear and fury. Who had done this?

He felt a hand on his back. He turned to look up at Nancy; tears were running down her cheeks.

"What happened?" His voice scraped through his tight throat.

"Len Dozier," Nancy said. "In a car. They came by and he…"

Eddie's father had also turned to look up at Nancy. She knelt down between them, hung her head down and whispered, "a broom."

That was enough. Eddie had heard of it, had known older Negro people who'd been struck by broom handles thrust from speeding cars. "Nigger-knocking," the rednecks called it. Eddie met his father's eyes. He knew it, too. He looked at Nancy. Even she knew about it, and he wondered if her tears were for Lakeesha or for the shame of her own race. At that moment, he wanted to push her away. He wanted no white person anywhere near his sister.

Nancy stood up, and backed away. Eddie thought she'd actually felt his hostility and moved away, but then he realized she had just made space for Coach Humphrey. Coach put two fingers gently on Lakeesha's throat, under her jaw, feeling for a pulse.

"She's alive," he said.

Eddie felt his father stiffen. If Lakeesha was alive, then they had to get her help, but how could they in this white world that had done this to his sister? Would anyone care? Would anyone help?

Coach Humphrey put his hand on Eddie's shoulder, but spoke to Reverend Russell. "You hang on, Reverend Russell. We'll get your baby to the hospital."

Coach Humphrey stood up. "Back off, boys, there's nothing to see here. You all go on back to the gym and make sure that Spencer has called for an ambulance."

But will you get the redneck that did this? Eddie thought.

"And the police," Coach Humphrey said. "Call the police."

Eddie watched the white boys' blank faces, saw Nancy sitting on the hood of Sally Hughes' baby-blue Mustang, her face in her hands. "Nancy Martin saw what happened," he said.

"So did I," said a quiet voice behind them. Eddie turned to see Clifford at the edge of the crowd with his Christmas camera in his hand.

CHAPTER 17

▼

TURN AWAY

Sunday evening, Eddie sat in a chair by Lakeesha's bed in the Negro wing of Baptist Hospital, praying for her to open her eyes and speak to him. He put his head down on the white sheet, breathing in the smell of alcohol and starch, the fainter smell of blood. He held her limp hand and rubbed her slim fingers. A broken bird, sleeping, her soul somewhere far away from them.

Reverend Russell and Eddie had slept for two nights on couches in the waiting room. The nurses had found them a couple of blankets and pillows, and had even let Reverend Russell sleep in an empty patient room for a couple of hours. But nothing could force his mother from Lakeesha's side. The only concession she had made to her own comfort had been to take her swollen feet out of her shoes. His father stood by the door, his mother on the other side of the bed.

Eddie and his father had left the hospital only briefly for church, where Reverend Russell had preached a one-minute sermon.

"My innocent daughter, my precious lamb, won't wake up. She can't talk to us. Senseless hate did this. Hate that has no place in this world. Pray for us, please, my brothers and sisters. Pray for all of us."

They left the congregation weeping and went back to the hospital room.

They all jumped at the soft tap on the door. Reverend Russell opened it a crack. "Eddie, someone to see you," he said.

Eddie placed Lakeesha's hand back on the sheet and went out into the hall. Spencer and Coach Humphrey were there at the front, and behind them Bobby Davidson and Steve Oakley, the whole starting team. Not quite, Eddie realized. Townsend wasn't there.

Spencer handed him a huge stuffed rabbit. They were all speaking, but Eddie was having trouble understanding what they were saying.

Coach Humphrey was talking to his father, handing him a big bunch of flowers. He heard his father saying, "…still hasn't regained consciousness."

The boys crowded close to Eddie, patting his back. He was speaking, not sure what exactly he was saying, things like, "Thanks," "We're waiting," "All we can do…"

Then they were leaving. Eddie was sorry to see them go, although he hadn't liked having them there, either. He could still feel the pressure of their hands on him, the comfort of their bodies close to him as he watched them walk down the hall and turn the corner toward the elevators. He clutched the stuffed rabbit, gently stroking its soft fur.

Eddie, still holding the rabbit, found his father down the hall in the waiting room, talking to the black doctors, a surgeon and a pediatric neurologist. Lakeesha had a severe concussion and possible internal injuries. Her nose had been shattered. A thick white bandage covered her nose, but not her eyes, which were swollen, stitched in several places and dark with bruises.

The doctors were arguing about whether Lakeesha should be operated on, to relieve pressure on her brain caused by internal swelling. The neurologist thought it was unnecessary, that it would subside soon. The surgeon, a younger man only a few years out of Meharry Medical School in Nashville, argued for more aggressive treatment. They agreed that the longer she lay in her coma, the more dangerous the situation became, the more likely she would have permanent damage. That was about all they agreed about.

They had sent the Russell's own family doctor, Dr. Gregg, packing on Saturday, completely dismissing him as an old fossil. Eddie left the doctors still arguing, revolted by their attitude. They were completely focused on each other, on winning their professional battle. Neither of them gave a flip about Lakeesha. They'd never seen her before in their lives. Not like Dr. Gregg, who'd been crying in church Sunday. His father listened without speaking, outwardly calm, but Eddie thought he was on the verge of either complete collapse or an explosion of monumental proportions.

Eddie got a cup of coffee at the nurses' station and took it into his mama. Her eyes were swollen and red, and when she took the cup of coffee he brought her, her hand shook.

The room was full of flowers, from everyone in their congregation it seemed, a big arrangement from the Martins, the basketball team's yellow and white 'mums. Eddie sat the big bunny on the windowsill. If Lakeesha ever opened her swollen eyes, that would be the first thing she saw, Eddie realized. She'd have to turn her head to see either her mother or her brother. Then Eddie realized that when his father was in the room, that was where he sat or stood, right in her line of sight. If she woke up she'd either see her father or a big white rabbit. He thought of putting a clerical collar on the bunny.

Eddie felt a burst of laughter build in his chest. His lips twitched. He looked over at his mother, whose eyes were closed. He had to get up and leave the room to laugh in the echoing hallway. A passing nurse patted his arm.

This is all my fault, he thought. *All my fault. I had to play the hero. Win at everything. Show I was as good as any white boy, better even. I knew Lakeesha would end up paying the price. My heart knew it.*

*   *   *   *

"Nan, it's Sally," her mother called up the stairs. Nancy rolled over and picked up the receiver. The rest of the blue princess phone fell off the bedside table and bounced on the floor.

"Hello?" she said, trying to wake up from a deep well of late afternoon sleep. She'd been sleeping a lot since Friday night.

"Hi, Nancy. Um, think you can get another ride to school tomorrow?"

"I guess so. Why?"

"Well, um, Daddy doesn't want me to give you rides anymore."

Nancy sat up, pulled the phone off the floor and put in on her lap, its numbers glowing in the semi-darkness.

"What?" *I must not be awake yet, she thought.*

"Well, um, that's what he says."

"But why?"

"He says you're a target, Nancy."

"A what? A target? For what?"

"For the kind of thing that happened the other night."

"But I didn't do anything."

"I know, but…"

"I helped somebody that was badly hurt, and your Daddy says you can't give me rides anymore?"

"Well, it isn't that simple, Nancy, and you know it. He's scared that Len Dozier's going to come after you again."

"They weren't coming after me the other night. They were coming after Lakeesha."

"That's what he won't understand. And besides, Len will be after you when you tell the police—"

"I already told them."

"See! He'll be after you."

"No, he won't. He'll be in jail."

"Daddy says they'll never arrest him."

"Why not? That's ridiculous. Clifford got a picture of him, clear as day."

"I told Daddy that, and he said I was being 'naïve.'"

"Naïve? What's that supposed to mean? That…doing that…I can't even say it."

"Well, you know as well as I do, Nancy, that more boys than Len Dozier go nigger-knocking."

Nancy winced.

Sally went on. "Even boys we associate with, not trash like Dozier, who you should never have messed with that day last fall at the smoking club. He's been eyeing you ever since. And then you and the colored girls had a fight with his girlfriend Kinsey the other day."

"We did not have a fight." Nancy would have laughed if the whole thing weren't so scary. "Sally! What did you expect me to do?"

"Your Daddy can give you a ride."

"I don't mean about a ride to school. I mean, do you expect me to just turn my back when things go on, pretend I don't see?"

Sally was silent, and Nancy realized the accusation she'd just made. Sally had never gotten out of her car the other night, not once, even when everyone else had been crowded around, waiting those long minutes for the ambulance to come, through the arguments with the white ambulance drivers about whether they'd take her, or whether they'd have to call a Negro ambulance, until Coach Humphrey had erupted in a rage and the white drivers had agreed to take Lakeesha to the hospital.

"Nancy, these people are beneath our notice." Sally's voice was cold. "And I don't mean trash like Kinsey Mackay and Len Dozier. I mean these colored kids."

"Oh, Eddie is now beneath our notice?"

"He's different, and even Eddie, it's not like we have to *socialize* with him."

"I don't…" Nancy stopped. She'd been about to deny she socialized with Eddie, and Lakeesha, and Lethe and Rochelle.

"You do too," Sally said. "You know you do, and everybody's talking about it. Everybody's talking about how you grabbed Eddie and how you had Lakeesha's blood all over you. And the whole Woodson team there watching!"

"So what? Eddie's sister was nearly killed, Sally. What was I supposed to do?"

"Nancy! Can't you see? You're too *involved*. People don't like it."

"So, what about you, Sally? You don't like it either?"

"Actually, no, I don't, Nancy."

Nancy's head felt like it had just exploded. Her hand moved, nearly slamming the phone down, but Sally beat her to it.

"Daddy's calling me. I'll see you," Sally said and clicked the phone down.

*   *   *   *

Monday morning, Nancy's father took her to school, and she walked in alone.

Missy and a few other senior girls chattered at the bottom of the stairs. Nancy walked toward them. Missy half-caught her eye and then turned and started up the stairs. The other seniors looked directly at Nancy, turned, and walked in different directions.

When they did, Nancy found herself face to face with Sally, who'd just come around the corner heading for homeroom. Sally stopped in her tracks. Her mouth half-opened, like she was going to speak, and then she turned around and walked away, disappearing around the corner.

Nancy's breath went out of her body in a rush. She felt people moving past her. Someone bumped into her and muttered an apology, but Nancy could hardly see. Light danced in front of her eyes and she thought she might be going to faint.

So, that's how it was going to be! Sally had warned her, but she could not believe this was happening. She had tried to help an injured human being. She'd thought everyone would praise her, pet her. Instead, she'd been marked. Why?

Nancy's eyes burned, and her throat clenched. She breathed in hard through her nose. She would *not* cry. Her head throbbed. She looked down at her feet. Then she spun around and ducked into the girls' bathroom. She hurried into a stall and closed the door. In the isolation of the cramped stall, she leaned her head against the cool metal door. Put her hands against it. Choked down sobs.

Other girls came in and out, toilets flushed, girls screamed with laughter and gossip. Nancy shut the sounds out. Her mind darted back to the day last fall in this very same bathroom, hearing sobs coming from behind a stall door. Was it this very one?

So this is how Lakeesha felt, Nancy thought.

✳ ✳ ✳ ✳

Nancy hesitated, looking across the cafeteria. In the middle of the echoing room, Missy looked at Nancy, narrowed her eyes and then looked away. Sally never even turned around.

Nancy felt her face tighten. She looked around desperately. Rochelle, who could always be counted on to lighten things up, was at the end of the snack line with some other tall, athletic girls.

Nancy crossed the short space between the door and the end of the teachers' table. She sank into a chair next to Lethe and sighed. Lethe was discussing a geometry problem with Sylvie Roberts, another sophomore brain. This earnest conversation with other students had become a regular part of lunch hour ever since Lethe had been inducted into the National Honor Society.

Sylvie packed up her books, and left the cafeteria. Rochelle headed for their table.

"What's wrong?" Rochelle asked as she sat down.

"Everything's changed." Nancy looked down at her hands clenched on the table.

"How? You mean Lakeesha? Have you heard anything?"

Nancy blushed. How could she be so worried about her own little problems when Lakeesha…

"Oh, no, it's nothing about that. It's not really that important, I guess. It's just that Missy and them aren't speaking to me." She couldn't admit that even Sally wouldn't speak to her.

"Why?" asked Lethe.

"I don't know. I don't get it."

"Sure you do!" Rochelle said. "You get it. It's clear as day. You got on the wrong side of the issue, girl. They'll make you pay for that. Not as bad as they made Lakeesha pay, but you're getting some of it."

"But I didn't do anything."

"Yes, you did. You're sitting here with us, aren't you, and not for the first time. You got Lakeesha's blood on you, didn't you? You touched Eddie right in front of the whole basketball team. You ratted on Len Dozier to the cops. You do the cheer for Eddie. You've gone to church with us. It's all built up, and now it's got you. They think you're dangerous."

"Me!" squeaked Nancy. "That's ridiculous."

Nancy saw Sally turn around, look at them and then quickly turn away.

"You're very dangerous, girl." Rochelle said. Her eyes looked tired and angry.

"So are we," said Lethe. Her jaw muscles jumped under the smooth dark skin of her cheeks. "Just being here makes us dangerous."

Just then Spencer burst through the swinging screen doors into the cafeteria and sat down beside Nancy. "Take a look at this." He handed Nancy a copy of the *Commercial-Appeal*. On the front were two pictures, one of Lakeesha being struck, the other of Len Dozier's face in the window of the car.

"Wow," Nancy said. "I guess they'll have to believe me now."

"About what?" asked Rochelle.

"That it was Len Dozier."

"What? They didn't believe you?" Spencer asked.

"No way. They sort of patted me on the head and told me to run away and play with my dollies."

Spencer looked at the pictures again. "Look, it's Clifford," he said, pointing to the credit line underneath. "He took these pictures. I didn't know that."

"That explains it."

"What?"

"I kept seeing bright lights flashing that night. I thought it was my imagination."

"He got that camera for Christmas," Lethe said.

Nancy looked at Rochelle, who was looking uncharacteristically uncertain. "What's wrong?"

"I don't know whether to tell you something."

"Well, now you have to. You can't bring something like that up and then not tell me."

"Clifford developed those pictures himself. The paper only took the best part of that one of the car, the clearest part."

Nancy looked bewildered. "Go on," she said.

"When you look at the whole picture, you can sort of see the driver, not very clear, but..." Rochelle said.

"But what?"

"You'll have to look at it yourself. I can bring you a copy."

"What?" Nancy asked. "Come on, Rochelle. Who was it?" And the minute she asked "Who," she knew.

"Larry Townsend," she and Rochelle said in unison.

CHAPTER 18

▼

BROKEN BIRD

On Monday morning, Eddie was back at Lakeesha's side after another night on the waiting room couch. He felt burnt out inside, his throat raw from sleeping in the room where other patients' worried families paced and smoked.

He had brought his mother a plate of eggs and biscuits, but she hadn't been able to eat it, had just taken the coffee. He chewed on the dry biscuit, hit a pocket of unmixed baking soda. His mother's biscuits never had anything like that.

Lakeesha's face still seemed to be swelling. Her eyes were barely visible, just slits in puffy flesh. No wonder she wouldn't wake up. She was far away from the pain now. Then he realized something. *She's far away from the pain*, he thought again. *No wonder she won't wake up*. If Mouse woke up she'd be back in the trap they'd set for her, from which she could not escape no matter which way she turned. They had left her no hole to disappear into. So she'd made one for herself.

And at that moment Eddie realized that Lakeesha was dying.

The realization was so powerful Eddie couldn't believe the whole room wasn't reverberating with a shout, but his mother looked just the same, her eyes closed, Lakeesha's hand in hers. She was asleep.

It was just past sunrise on a clear, cool March morning. His father wasn't in the room. He was probably still asleep on the couch in the waiting room. The whole hospital seemed still, holding its breath, waiting for Lakeesha to die.

Eddie knelt by Lakeesha's side and took her other hand in his, stroked it, then leaned forward and put his mouth next to her ear. "Don't leave us, Keesha. Please, please, please don't leave us. I will find a way to get you out of this. Come back and you will be safe. I swear to you, Keesha. You are my sister and I will protect you."

He leaned his head down on the sheets next to her arm and reviewed the whole horrible year. He'd been fighting the whole time, angry every minute, pushing and scratching and clawing for respect, recognition. He'd had nothing to spare for his defenseless sister. The tears began to leak from his eyes and his shoulders shook.

What could he do to save her? He froze as it came to him as inevitable as the sun rising in the morning. "You have to be like Gandhi," the words came back to him. "Like Gandhi."

Eddie stood up and let go Lakeesha's hand, placing it carefully on the white sheet. He looked at her and turned to go find his father, to jump off the mountain.

Reverend Russell was in the waiting room, alone, looking out the wire-reinforced window into a parking lot below. He seemed small, ill, old. Eddie almost lost his nerve.

"Dad?"

His father turned around. His eyes were red, as if he'd been crying, but his face was calm. He didn't speak.

"Dad, it was wrong to ask Lakeesha to do this. I've always known it was wrong. I wanted to say so right from the beginning but—"

"I know, son. She has paid for my selfishness, my egotism. I wanted to be respected, to be a leader in the black community. Willing to sacrifice my own children to this 'righteous cause' of mine. How righteous can any cause be that is built on the suffering of children?" He turned back to the window and then suddenly grabbed the window sill and said, "Oh, God help us!" in a strangled voice and began to sob, his shoulders shaking.

Eddie came to his father, gripped his shoulders, then wrapped his arms around him.

"I'm to blame, too, Dad. I've been going through school like a thunder storm, every day, daring anybody to put me down. I was trying so hard to prove I was somebody. That made things worse. Lakeesha's the one who paid."

His father breathed in hard, trying to compose himself.

"Dad, I'm not going to play basketball anymore. I'm too angry. I'm drawing too much attention to myself. I think I should go more softly now."

His father nodded and patted Eddie's hand.

"And Lakeesha…"

"Is not going back," his father said. "Whether she lives or leaves us, she will never go back to that school."

"You should go tell her that."

His father turned and looked at Eddie in astonishment. "Tell her?"

"Yes, I'm sure she can hear us. I'm afraid she doesn't want to come back."

*   *   *   *

Monday night, Reverend Russell sent Eddie and his wife out of the room and sat by Lakeesha's side for more than an hour, talking to her quietly, holding her hand. Confessing, Eddie thought.

On Tuesday morning, Lakeesha opened her eyes.

When her eyelids flickered, Eddie stopped breathing. Mama made a tiny whimpering sound. His father clutched the metal rail on the end of the bed.

Then her eyes opened and she looked straight at her father, her hands held by Eddie and her mother. She gave Eddie's hand the tiniest squeeze. Tears began to roll down his mother's cheeks. She lifted Lakeesha's hand and kissed it over and over again, saying, "My baby, my baby." Lakeesha's eyes flicked toward her mother and then toward Eddie.

Her mother began kissing Lakeesha all over her face, ignoring the bandages across her nose. Lakeesha whispered something they couldn't understand, her voice rough and dry. Eddie rang and rang on the emergency call button. Then the nurses were there, hustling them aside while they spoke to Lakeesha, took her blood pressure, called the doctors.

In the dusty waiting room, stale with cigarette smoke, they all knelt to pray.

That afternoon, Eddie left the hospital for the first time since Sunday, when he and his father had gone to church. The doctors were ecstatic, especially the pediatric neurologist, who'd won the battle by default since the patient had awakened before they'd argued the case for surgery to conclusion. They had been so euphoric they'd even called Dr. Gregg back in, and he too had wept over the patient. After all, he had delivered her, immunized her, given her penicillin for throat infections, and bounced her on his knee at church picnics.

Mama was even more firmly rooted to the chair by Lakeesha's bed now that her baby was awake, but in the evening she persuaded Eddie and Reverend Russell to get out of the hospital for a while.

Being out in the fresh March air woke Eddie up; his spirits soared on the wind. The image of Lakeesha's eyes opening, the faint pressure of her hand on his came to him again and again. He had never felt so free, so light. His anger was gone, his hate was gone. Everything had changed. He loved his father, walking so carefully beside him. He loved Lakeesha, who'd come back to them from the edge of that dark land. He loved his mother, who held on no matter what.

He thought of Spencer and Mr. Young, and Fletcher and the bookcase. He remembered all the anger he'd carried through the halls at Forrest and shook his head in wonder that he'd managed to make any friends at all.

"What's the matter, son?" his father asked.

But the laughter just bubbled up and out. Eddie put his arm around his father. "Nothing, Dad. I have looked into the heart of my enemy and found something to love."

CHAPTER 19

▼

YOU KNOW SOMETHING'S HAPPENING

On April first, three weeks after Lakeesha awakened and two weeks after the last basketball game, cheerleading tryouts for the next year were held.

Nancy had faced a panel of cheerleading judges six times now, beginning in the seventh grade. She had three stars on the arm of her cheerleading sweater for each year she'd been a high school cheerleader. She only needed the fourth to make it a clean sweep.

This year the judges looked very serious: Two athletes, Townsend and Spencer; Miss Thoreau, the only one laughing; Coach Ezell; Coach Humphrey; Mrs. Granger; sophomore Lynn Monahan and junior Wayne Rogers representing students. A pack of other students crowded into the balcony, but even they were unusually quiet. Nancy spotted Eddie, Fletcher, Bobby Davidson, Steve Oakley and Sam Jones.

She waited on the stage of the auditorium with the first group of six candidates, ready to smile her hardest and jump her highest when Missy gave the signal. But another part of her seemed to be floating somewhere in the balcony, looking down at herself, finding her behavior slightly ridiculous. Nancy shook her head and tried to focus.

Missy looked so happy there on the floor of the auditorium, right next to the stage. She would be graduating in May. She had cheered for her last game and was ready to pass the torch. Nancy wondered what Missy would do with herself in college if she couldn't be a cheerleader. Nothing suited her so well as being a cheerleader, bossing other cheerleaders. She would probably make cheerleader at Ole Miss, where she was going, but what on earth would she do with herself after college?

Now Missy put on her game smile and tapped her foot, ready to direct the try-outs. She raised her arm and let it fall. In unison, the candidates for cheerleader broke into a chant, flinging their arms up and down and side to side.

> *We're the champs,*
> *(clap, clap.)*

Nancy thought, "He's a jinx…" and momentarily missed a beat. She caught herself quickly, so quickly she was sure, really sure, no one had noticed. She smiled as hard as she could.

*   *   *   *

Eddie came into the balcony of the auditorium just as the first group of cheerleading candidates stood poised on the stage, ready for the signal to begin. He sat down a little apart from the rest of the students, who hung over the railing on the front row.

He'd been back in school since the day after Lakeesha had opened her eyes. That first morning he'd grabbed his jacket unconsciously, pulled it on before he stopped and thought maybe he didn't need armor anymore. He'd hung it back on its hook and walked out, feeling naked. But no one had even seemed to notice. He'd gotten through the worst of the questions, the speculation and the accusations about his quitting the basketball team. And he was amazed how easy it had been, how little he cared.

Lakeesha had just come home from the hospital that week. She looked tired and thin, but her eyes glowed with contentment, to be home with her family, her friends and her books. She wouldn't leave the house. The porch was as far as she'd go, and no one seemed inclined to force the issue. Maybe on Sunday, they'd try to get her to church, but for now, Lakeesha was having everything her own way. Ice cream, fried chicken, whatever she wanted. The doctors said there was a possibility of complications if she had any stress at all and that she could not return to school that year. No one had raised a single objection to that.

Now Eddie wanted to see how things would come out for Nancy Martin. She seemed to be catching more grief than he was. All her friends were still ignoring her.

Eddie missed the signal and suddenly the cheerleaders were jumping on the stage. He leaned forward.

> *We're the champs,*
> *(clap, clap.)*

Eddie stiffened. He knew the alternate version, *"He's a jinx, clap, clap."* He watched Nancy and saw her moment of hesitation. Then she was back moving smoothly through the cheer. Eddie wondered what had caused the hitch.

*   *   *   *

"Well, Mom, I didn't make cheerleader." Nancy dropped her books on the kitchen table and sat down.

"Oh, no, honey," her mother wailed.

Hattie hurried into the kitchen from the laundry room where she had been finishing up the ironing. Nancy could smell the steaming cotton. As long as Nancy could remember, Hattie had been there to comfort her in her troubles, hug her when she scraped her knees, bring her soup when she had the flu, heap insults on her ex-boyfriends. As much a mother to her as her own mother. She was glad they were both there.

"I've never liked the way they pick the cheerleaders one bit," Hattie said. "It's purely a popularity contest!"

Nancy looked from one anxious face to the other and forced herself to laugh. "It's not the end of the world." She would *not* cry.

Her father walked through the door, stripping off his suit coat and tossing it on the back of a chair. He'd been taking her to school and picking her up ever since the night Lakeesha had been attacked. Nancy flat refused to take the bus.

"What happened, darling?" her mother said. Her father loosened his tie and sat down at the table across from them.

"I don't know. Maybe my heart wasn't really in it today. I didn't feel the same way I always have before. Maybe it showed. I started thinking of something else right in the middle of a cheer." She shook her head in disbelief.

"Maybe it's because you too good friends with Lakeesha and Lethe, Rochelle, the colored girls," Hattie said. "You know a lot of people don't like that one bit."

They all looked uncomfortably at Hattie. "Hattie, I didn't want to say that, but I think, I think..." She tried to smile, but her mother and Hattie rushed over and started patting her. Her father laughed, and both women shot him hard looks.

"Stop glaring at me," her father said. "You two are the worst mother hens I've ever seen."

Nancy snorted with suppressed laughter that was dangerously close to tears.

Hattie put a freshly ironed handkerchief in her hand. The phone rang. It was Spencer.

＊   ＊   ＊   ＊

"I feel lost," Nancy said as they whirled down the highway.

"Aw, it doesn't matter," Spencer said.

"I've always been a cheerleader."

"It doesn't matter. At all!"

"Doesn't it?" She leaned her head against the glass of the window. "You know what it's been like. All my friends have turned against me because I've been friends with the Negro kids. Ever since that night Lakeesha got hurt, but really it started before that. You know Sally has stopped picking me up. Her father won't let her. He said I was a target for people like Len Dozier. They think I'm different now. Not the kind of person a cheerleader should be."

Spencer pulled the car off the road and turned off the engine. He turned to her, leaning back against the door. She leaned against the opposite door and pulled her feet up onto the seat.

"Well, aren't they right? Aren't you different?"

Nancy sat back, her eyes unfocused, and her eyebrows pulled together in concentration. "Yes, I guess I am."

"Are you sorry? Would you change it?"

"No," she said, finally. "I wouldn't change a thing I've done this year."

Spencer didn't say anything.

Nancy smiled, though her lips quivered. "I bet I won't get elected to a class office for next year either. I'm up for president but that was before...Those teachers, they must have voted against me."

"It wasn't just them."

Of course! He knew why they hadn't chosen her. She'd forgotten he had been one of the judges. "Who was it?" she asked slowly, the answer coming to her as soon as she asked the question.

Spencer looked away from her, out at the road where a few cars whipped by.

"Go on. Tell me. Larry, right? But he only had one vote."

"Yeah, it was Townsend. Some of the teachers thought you had too much already. The coaches were worried that you were too 'controversial.' But Townsend, he iced it. He said you weren't 'a good representative of Forrest' anymore. That seemed to sum it up."

"Larry!" Spots fluttered before her eyes. She was so mad she nearly threw up.

Spencer looked at her. "Yeah, Larry."

Nancy looked out the window at a house with a tire swing hanging from a big tree.

Spencer reached across and pulled her to his chest, patting her back and kissing her head. She didn't cry.

"I'll kill him for you," Spencer said.

Nancy laughed into Spencer's sweatshirt. "You can't; he's too popular."

*   *   *   *

Just how popular Larry was they found out the next day. Mrs. Granger called Nancy and five other "outstanding juniors" to an after-school meeting. All the class officers were there, plus April Rawlins, vice-president of the National Honor Society, and Bobby Davidson, vice-president of the "F" Club, the athletic honor society.

Mrs. Granger told them they had been chosen to make speeches at the Senior Honors Banquet, to sing the praises of Forrest High School's six most outstanding seniors.

"Nancy, your senior is Larry Townsend," Mrs. Granger said brightly. She beamed at Nancy, who turned pale, seeing a spark of malice in Mrs. Granger's big blue eyes. Bobby looked at Nancy curiously. Nancy saw the avid look and gritted her teeth, forcing herself to smile.

"The banquet is only a week from tonight, so work hard on those speeches! I know you'll all do a simply wonderful job. And maybe this time next year, you'll be the ones who are honored." Mrs. Granger waggled her head at them.

As Nancy walked out the front doors of the school, Wayne Rogers caught up with her.

"Nancy!"

She turned around slowly.

"Nancy, I'll switch with you if you want. I, uh, get the impression you don't like Larry very much."

Nancy looked into Wayne's worried eyes behind the glasses.

"Thanks, Wayne. I guess I'll just try to get through it, but you're right. I don't like Larry much anymore."

Awkwardly, Wayne patted her shoulder.

Nancy turned and hurried to the car where her mother waited.

When Nancy got home, she slowly walked upstairs to her room. She yanked out *Highway 61 Revisited* and slammed it onto the record player. She popped the needle down onto "Ballad of a Thin Man" and sang along, pacing.

> *Oh, my God, am I here all alone?*
> *Well, you know something's happening*
> *But you don't know what it is,*
> *Do you, Mr. Jones?*

An hour of Dylan later, she slumped exhausted in her blue-and-white chair. Her head dropped back; her eyes closed. Her fingers tapped the arm, then tapped slower. Her eyes opened, narrowing. She smiled. Then she laughed, jumped up, grabbed a pen, opened her notebook, and began to write her speech.

＊　　　＊　　　＊　　　＊

On the first Friday in May, Nancy stepped up to the podium after April finished her speech about Vicki Fitzpatrick, outgoing senior class president. Juniors, seniors, teachers, parents packed the cafeteria. The school year was racing to its end. The seniors were already having all kinds of special days, and graduation practices and awards ceremonies. It had gotten hot, too, in the last few days, and the cafeteria held the day's heat, so that Nancy's back itched from sweat. She should have worn a cooler dress.

She hesitated a moment, nailing the first line of her speech back down for the thousandth time in her mind. She took a deep breath and pulled the microphone down, then down some more, made a face and laughed.

"April's so tall," she said, her voice echoing back to her from the public address system. Everyone laughed.

Nancy was the last to speak. Larry sat on the front row, his eyes riveted on her. She smiled down at him, savoring it.

"What makes an outstanding senior?" Nancy paused, looked around as if waiting for an answer. The whole speech flowed from that line, smooth and even. "I think we all know. I think we would all agree about what makes a person a fine human being, a person we can honor and respect. A person who will go out into the world from Forrest High School and make us proud. Who will be recognized instantly as fine and fair and true as steel.

"Outstanding," she paused, looking out over the faces. She felt Larry's stare on her like a blowtorch.

"What makes a person outstanding?" she repeated. She looked down at Spencer, whose face was puzzled and apprehensive.

"An outstanding person never thinks of himself," Nancy said quietly, as if thinking aloud. "He puts others ahead of himself. He thinks of the team before he thinks of himself. He doesn't try to grab glory, but success just comes to that kind of person." She saw Mr. Young sitting next to Mrs. Odetts. They had their heads together, whispering.

"Outstanding." She looked around, catching Missy's eye. Missy was frowning, tapping her foot nervously on the front row.

"An outstanding person is kind, right to the core of his being. Kind, gentle, strong, defending those weaker than he, a support for those who are already strong." She looked around, caught Coach Ezell's eye. He was frowning, too.

"An outstanding person is never harsh or violent or hurtful. An outstanding person accepts others, with understanding and tolerance for their differences." She caught Miss Thoreau's eye and was thrown off for a moment because the gym teacher was laughing and punching Coach Humphrey, who also grinned wickedly.

"An outstanding person is surrounded by friends, loved by everyone for the way his soul shines and warms everyone around him."

"An outstanding person always knows the right thing to do, never does things that would dishonor him. He defends the defenseless. He stands with his friends, adding his strength to theirs."

She looked around, smiling brilliantly, and caught Eddie's eye. Eddie flashed her a thumbs up. She smiled down at Larry, whose face was pasty white, deep lines etched into either side of his mouth. Their eyes locked for a long moment.

Then she looked out over the crowd, smiling like a saint.

"I won't go on and on. I think everyone here knows whether Larry 'Touchdown' Townsend, the captain of the football team and the basketball team, is that kind of person, an outstanding person, a person we can love and respect and wish well. Congratulations, Larry!"

Nancy's legs shook. The applause was hearty, but ripples of laughter and angry comment shot through it. Larry slowly stalked onto the dais, toward Nancy. Her heart stopped at the murderous look in his icy eyes.

I went too far, she thought in a panic. *He'll kill me now, for sure.*

He stopped before her, one step too close. She backed up. He bent his blond head. Standing on her tiptoes, Nancy dropped the ribbon with its medal over his head. Her fingers touched him, and she almost snatched her hands away, the ripple of repressed rage was so intense.

As his head came up, he moved his mouth away from the microphone and whispered, "Bitch." Not far enough. The word crackled a little but was plain to everyone in the room. Hundreds of families, friends, teachers, and students gasped, then some of them tittered.

Larry's eyes dropped away from Nancy's, a murky red staining his cheeks. The skin at the corners of his mouth was white.

She realized with a shock that she had won. She looked at Spencer and smiled. He grinned back. Then Eddie. The triumphant grin on his face surprised her, inspired her.

"Why, Larry." She half-turned so the microphone picked it up clearly. "I meant every word I said."

Laughter chased Larry as he hurried down the stairs.

"Just not about you," she whispered to herself, looking at Spencer.

CHAPTER 20

▼

WE KISSED IN
THE WILD
BLAZING
NIGHTIME

It was Friday, the third week of May. Only one more week of school. Monday was the seniors' last real day of school. They spent the first part of next week in special assemblies, and then graduated on Thursday.

Home room was extended because yearbooks were being distributed. Miss Cross was opening one of the two boxes on her desk and calling out names. Eddie didn't quite understand why everyone was bouncing in their seats and jabbering. He waited calmly for his name to be called. All around him as people got their yearbooks, they flipped to the first two pages of the class sections. A violent buzz broke out, which Miss Cross made no attempt to contain. Then suddenly Steve Oakley, one of the first to get his book, turned around and yelled across the room to him, "Hey! Eddie! You're a Best Athlete."

An eruption of chatter, and then a cheer. Spencer turned around and cuffed him on the shoulder.

"Hey! Spence! You too!" Oakley called across the room, and everyone cheered.

Then Eddie's name was called, and he went up to get his royal blue and gold yearbook, brining it back to his seat. He watched where everyone else was opening their books and flipped to the two pages at the beginning of the junior section. There it was. Wayne Rogers and Kathy Perkins were Mr. and Miss Junior. April Rawlins and Steve Oakley were Best Scholars. Cindy Yoder was most Beautiful, Bobby Davidson was Most Handsome. Sally Hughes and Bobby Davidson were Most Popular. And there were Spencer Smith and Eddie Russell, Best Athletes. The entire class had voted for these honors months ago, but Eddie hadn't paid much attention.

Suddenly Rochelle's voice cut through the hubbub. "Hey!" she said. "Hasn't there ever in the history of the world been a girl voted Best Athlete?"

Just then, as everyone laughed, the bell rang. Eddie, still in a daze, gathered his books and yearbook and headed out the door, almost colliding with Larry in the hallway. As he backed away, Marvin Fletcher came racing up, pounding on Eddie.

"Congratulations, Eddie."

Other people surrounded him, someone clapped him on the back and called him, "Mr. Touchdown."

Eddie lifted his eyes to Townsend's. Fletcher followed his gaze.

"Oh, hi, Larry. Hey, don't be mad. You'll always be Touchdown Townsend, but Eddie's *Mr.* Touchdown."

*   *   *   *

"Hey, look at this! You are not going to believe it," April Rawlins gasped.

April, standing on a chair to hold ropes of crepe paper high off the floor, had her nose pressed against the window. Kathy Perkins and Nancy kept on twisting crepe paper to decorate the gym for the Junior Prom. The community room was wedged between the girls' gym and the New Building. Its windows looked straight into the cosmetology department, if you were standing on a chair.

"April! You're stretching it." Kathy grabbed the crepe paper away from April.

"What is it?" Nancy hopped up on a chair beside April and peered through the window.

"Wow!" she breathed. Framed in the window stood Mr. Young, wrapped in a pink flowered hairdresser's cape, his head slick with black dye. He stood with one foot up on a reclining chair, his arms outstretched, his mouth moving furiously. They could see the back of Mrs. Odetts' dark stiff hair. Mr. Young made a final flourish of his arms and bowed. Mrs. Odetts' hands moved as if she were clapping. April and Nancy looked at each other in amazement and then burst into laughter.

Kathy jumped up on a chair, dropping the pink and blue crepe paper in a heap, but Mr. Young had moved offstage and was invisible now.

"What?" she asked. "What was it?"

"Mr. Young…" Nancy was laughing too hard to continue.

When April, stuttered out what they'd seen, Kathy said, "Oh, he's in Little Theater. That's all he was doing, just practicing his part."

April and Nancy looked at each other, then burst into laughter. Today, everything they did was funny. No more classes. The Junior Prom tonight, and then on Monday, just assemblies and report cards. They'd go home at noon.

Just then Cindy dashed in. "Listen! You know what? Larry Townsend got his draft notice!"

"You're kidding!" Kathy said. "Boy, they didn't even wait for graduation."

"He's 18," April said. "That's all that matters to them."

"Oh, he'll get out of it. He's going to college. They'll never get Touchdown Townsend to Vietnam," Cindy said.

They all looked at Nancy. She was silent, looking down.

"You know, Nancy, you probably did him a lot of good with that speech," April said. "I've been meaning to tell you that. It was…well, he deserved it."

"Yeah," said Cindy. "He's just been getting more and more mean and arrogant every year. Somebody needed to bring him down."

"Right," said Kathy. "I wanted to tell you that, too."

Nancy blushed. "Thanks," she said.

"And, while we're at it, I want to apologize for how I've been about the colored students. I was horrible about the tapping. Wayne's been after me about it ever since."

Nancy looked at April, a faint smile only in her eyes. April saw it.

"Thanks, Kathy," said Nancy. "I'm glad."

*   *   *   *

The Russells' living room was crowded with adults, arguing.

On the porch outside, Lethe, Lakeesha and Rochelle were squeezed onto the swing, looking in through the window into the living room with every swish forward. Eddie leaned against the railing.

Inside, Mr. Collier and Mr. Reed sat on kitchen chairs facing the couch, and the window. Reverend Russell sat in his faded wing chair by the door. Mr. Jefferson, Mrs. Russell and Mrs. Perry were jammed uncomfortably on the deep couch.

"Dr. King would say the Movement needs patience and love, not the anger I am hearing," they heard Reverend Russell say.

"The Movement is changing," Mr. Reed said harshly. "We are moving on. Black Power is where we need to go, forget this trying to be *like* white people, *with* white people."

"You young people from SNCC are playing with the lives of our children," Mr. Jefferson said. "I saw the justification for what we asked them to do this year. I still do. They have had some stellar successes. You should not try to undo all that on some whim."

"It's no whim," Mr. Reed insisted. "Some of us have finally lost patience. It's time to push harder for our rights."

"The only way we'll ever achieve integration is if we can get more than just one or two or four black children in those white schools," Mr. Collier said. "That's going to take lawsuits."

"It's going to take busing," said Mr. Reed.

"Other black children will be at Forrest next year. They will follow in the path these children have laid down," said Mr. Jefferson.

The argument had been going on for nearly half an hour.

Rochelle pushed the swing again with her foot.

"Well, if they let *us* decide, I'm going back to Douglass. No question," she said. "I ain't had a moment's peace at that school. I want to be with my own people. This integration is never going to work."

Eddie smiled at her.

"I'm going to the prom with you tonight, Eddie, but that's the last time I'll go out of my way to get white people to 'accept' me. I still think you should of asked Etta Lee. She's crazy about you, and you know it."

"No, she's not used to it like you are. It's our junior prom, Rochelle. We should go together."

Rochelle's mouth curled up, but she kept quiet.

Eddie looked at Lakeesha, waiting for her to speak. Lakeesha was almost well. All her bandages were off, and she was going to church again. She'd missed the last three months of school, and they had agreed she could go to summer school at Douglass to make it up. She spoke firmly.

"I'm going back to Douglass."

Eddie opened his mouth.

"No, don't interrupt me," Lakeesha said. "If I went back, things might be better now at Forrest, it's true. But I've always wanted to go back to Douglass. Other kids are going to take my place there this year; Etta Lee's going, but I want to be someplace where I'm loved."

"You going to be able to stand up to your daddy? Tell him that?" Rochelle asked.

"Yes, I am," Lakeesha said.

Eddie let his breath out. He hadn't told anyone about his conversation with their father in the hospital. Their father would never be able to deny Lakeesha anything, ever again. But Lakeesha shouldn't be denied the triumph of telling him what she wanted, and getting her own way.

"Well, I'm staying at Forrest," Lethe said. "It's simply a better school. I plan to go to Vassar or Radcliffe. They wouldn't even *look* at my application if I stayed at Douglass."

Then they all looked at Eddie, and Rochelle said, "So, Steady Eddie, how 'bout you?"

He closed his eyes for a minute, trying to find the words.

"I'll stay at Forrest," he said at last.

Rochelle hooted.

"Will you play football again?" Lethe asked.

Eddie hesitated, thought about it. "I will if I feel like I can keep it under control. If I can play like I played at Douglass, for the joy in it, instead of making it some kind of war for acceptance."

"Why don't you just go back to Douglass then?" Rochelle asked. "That way you'll know you're just playing for fun."

"I don't know, I feel like if I went back to Douglass I'd just be going through the motions, going to school, getting up in the morning. At Forrest, every time someone smiles at me it's a victory."

"So, you feel significant," Lethe said.

Eddie grinned. "You got it. That's exactly what I mean. I feel significant."

"So you haven't completely gone Gandhi on us," Rochelle said with a wicked grin.

Eddie was shocked. Was he so transparent? He thought all that had just been between him and God.

The girls all laughed. "Eddie, we all knew what you were doing," said Lethe. "We think you're great. You've done the right thing, but I think the self-sacrifice thing has run its course."

"Now," Rochelle stood up and put her hands on the porch window sash. "Shall we tell them?"

"Yes," said Lethe and Eddie in unison.

Rochelle threw open the window into the living room. The adults all stopped talking, their mouths open in surprise.

"Why don't you all stop arguing about what we ought to do and ask us?" Rochelle said.

There was a shocked silence, and then Rochelle mother's laughed. "She's right. We should hear these children out. They the one's been paying the price."

Mr. Reed looked furious but kept his mouth shut. They all left the porch and trooped into the living room, standing in a ragged row facing the adults.

"All right," Reverend Russell said. "What have you children decided?"

"I'll go back to Forrest." Eddie said.

"I will too," Lethe said.

"I'm going back to Douglass," Rochelle said. Mr. Reed gave a little cheer.

They all looked at Lakeesha. She held her chin up, squared her shoulders and said clearly, "I'm going back to Douglass."

Their father looked at the ground and did not speak. But Mama stood up and came to Lakeesha. She held out her arms, and Lakeesha stepped into a hug that made Eddie's throat close up.

"Good girl," Mama said. "That's my girl."

*   *   *   *

Nancy twirled in front of her mirror. A daring dress, she thought, amazed her mother had let her buy it. Gold, tight, short, the low-cut bodice encrusted with transparent gold bangles. She twirled again, admiring how the fringe of bangles flared. Her earrings dangled, and her high-heeled sandals twinkled in the lamp-lit room.

On Friday the class offices had been announced. Wayne Rogers was the new class president. Her own reaction had surprised her. She had felt hurt and embarrassed at first, but then slowly she felt a strange sense of relief, of freedom. She suddenly saw the possibilities of being on the outside of the inner circle. She had written off to New York University for a catalog and application. She marveled at all the free time she would have. She twirled again and grinned at herself in the mirror. This dress was an even prettier gold than the pleats in her old cheerleading uniform.

The doorbell rang. Blondie barked. She heard Spencer and her father. Their voices rumbled, and then they laughed. A friendship had sprung up between them, although her mother still always managed to get in a dig about him whenever Spencer called or came over.

Nancy ruffled her short red hair. She had had it cut only two hours ago. She put one last dot of lipstick on, adjusted the spaghetti straps of her dress and danced downstairs. Spencer was talking to her Dad, a box in his hand. He stopped abruptly when he saw her. His eyebrows shot up.

"Wow! You look great!" he said, holding out the box that held a pink and white orchid. Her mother came in and took the orchid, but had a hard time finding enough dress to pin the flower to.

As they left the house, Nancy felt like she was dancing on the crest of an ocean wave. They drove to the gym with the radio at top volume, laughing at everything, singing *"You don't have to say you love me,"* along with Dusty Springfield.

As they walked across the dark parking lot toward the gym, Nancy grabbed Spencer's arm in its black tuxedo jacket and twinkled around him like a sprite. They could hear voices and the throb of a band. They crossed the street and ducked under two thick cypress trees that hung over the back sidewalk to the gym. Nancy's dress sparkled in the bright moonlight. Spencer pulled her toward him and kissed her. Nancy kissed him back. He pulled her closer, kissing her again.

She leaned into his arms. Spencer suddenly picked her up and carried her toward the gym. Nancy's legs kicked furiously as they rounded the corner. The kids hanging around the door to the gym laughed and clapped.

Spencer gently put Nancy down and hand-in-hand they went into the gym. Miss Cross beamed at the students who passed the door. She reached out and took Nancy's hand, leaning toward her so that her lips touched Nancy's ear. The music was so loud, she couldn't have been heard otherwise.

"My dear, I'm proud of the way you've handled yourself these past few months, especially your speech at the honors banquet."

Miss Cross leaned back and smiled.

Spencer pulled at her. Nancy grabbed Miss Cross's hands and said, "Thank you, Miss Cross, thank you so much for telling me that."

Nancy glowed as she and Spencer moved toward the dance floor until Sally appeared right in front of her. They hadn't spoken to each other for three months. Sally's pale skin flushed, but she met Nancy's eyes and did not move.

"I've been wanting to be friends again for so long, but I was embarrassed," Sally quavered. "It just got started, because Missy got mad at you, and I just couldn't…"

"I understand," Nancy said. She had imagined this moment for a long time, rehearsed so many replies that she'd worn herself out. Now that Sally was actually speaking to her, she really didn't feel anything except cold inside, embarrassed, wanting to get away. She'd imagined them being friends again in some of her fantasies, but now she wondered.

Then Bobby Davidson grabbed Sally's hand and pulled her toward the dance floor. Sally dashed the tears out of her eyes with the back of her hand and followed him.

Nancy spun around to Spencer. He led her onto the floor. The band was a 10-piece Negro orchestra in powder blue tuxedos, with three lead singers in white tuxes.

Just as Nancy and Spencer hit the dance floor the band's base guitarist strummed the throbbing first notes of The Temptations hit, "My Girl."

Bah, bom, bom, Bah, bom, bom.

Spencer grabbed Nancy's waist, took her hand and twirled her in a complicated spin. Their feet flashed across the floor, and people moved back, giving them room, watching their swinging moves. Soon only one other couple was still on the dance floor with them—Eddie and Rochelle.

They became aware of each other and dipped and swayed in time, grinning at each other. Nancy stared at Rochelle, who had cut her hair off short too. It fluffed out around her head in the first Afro that Nancy or anyone else at Forrest High School had ever seen.

Eddie twirled the lean Rochelle in her tight white satin dress, singing along with the band.

Nancy sang too, and Spencer croaked the words into her hair.

"My girl," they all sang together, leaning toward each other, like the singers in the band did. "My girl!"

Then Spencer cocked his eyebrows at Eddie. "How 'bout it, Mr. Touchdown? Want to switch?"

Eddie nodded, unable to speak. He whirled Rochelle toward Spencer and then Nancy Martin was in his arms, his hands were holding hers.

Eddie placed his hand on Nancy's waist. He squeezed her hand, and they twirled and dipped as one person. Eddie thought they were better matched than she and Spencer, who was so much taller.

Her hand was softer than Rochelle's or even Etta Lee's. Eddie abandoned himself to the music and the dangerous delight of holding a white girl, this girl, in his arms in front of everyone.

The band played to their dancing now, drawing the relatively short song out, longer and longer, replaying the instrumental riffs and starting the verses over again.

Eddie looked over at the teachers against the wall, all watching them dancing. Mrs. Granger looked like she'd bitten into a bad egg. Mr. Young beamed at them, his fat cheeks a brilliant red.

Eddie felt as high as a skyrocket, his eyes catching the flecks of gold from Nancy's dress as the trumpets moaned. Eddie twirled her from one end of the dance floor to the other, his lean legs and her gold sandals moving in time to the full orchestra. Scattered clapping, mixed with a few boos, broke out in the crowd.

Then Spencer was by his side, wanting his date back. With a wrench, Eddie let Nancy go.

Then Rochelle was back, and Eddie whirled her down the floor so fast she laughed and had to hang onto his arms.

With one last crashing chord, the song ended and together Eddie, Rochelle, Spencer and Nancy bowed to each other, sweeping their arms out to one side.

71881121R00103

Made in the USA
Lexington, KY
25 November 2017